TIME VILLAINS

VICTOR PIÑEIRO

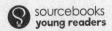

Published by Sourcebooks Young Readers, an imprint of Sourcebooks Kids
P.O. Box 4410, Naperville, Illinois 60567-4410
(630) 961-3900
sourcebookskids.com

Library of Congress Cataloging-in-Publication Data
Names: Piñeiro, Victor, author.
Title: Time villains / Victor Piñeiro.
Description: Naperville, Illinois : Sourcebooks Young Readers, [2021] |
  Audience: Ages 8 and up. | Audience: Grades 4-6. | Summary: When a
  homework assignment and a magic table summon real and fictional people
  from history, including the bloodthirsty pirate Blackbeard, sixth-grader
  Javi, his brawny younger sister Brady, and his brainy best friend Wiki
  join forces to save the world.
Identifiers: LCCN 2021000990 (print) | LCCN 2021000991 (ebook)
Subjects: CYAC: Time travel--Fiction. | Magic--Fiction. |
  Supernatural--Fiction. | Blackbeard, d. 1718--Fiction. |
  Pirates--Fiction. | Puerto Ricans--Fiction.
Classification: LCC PZ7.1.P559 Ti 2021 (print) | LCC PZ7.1.P559 (ebook) |
  DDC [Fic]--dc23
LC record available at https://lccn.loc.gov/2021000990
LC ebook record available at https://lccn.loc.gov/2021000991

Source of Production: Maple Press, York, Pennsylvania, United States
Date of Production: May 2021
Run Number: 5021585

Printed and bound in the United States of America.
MA 10 9 8 7 6 5 4 3 2 1

To Evelyn, for everything

1

We found the table in some weird antique flea market. Our old dining room table was busted, so we were looking for a new one, but Dad didn't want to take us to some regular furniture store. No, Dad loves taking Brady and me to super-boring places on the weekends because he thinks torture is healthy for kids. Mostly it's museums and the symphony and other stuff designed to make us die of boredom, but when he's really feeling diabolical, he takes us to antique stores, so we can look at combs and toilets from a hundred years ago. Usually I drag my feet and moan the whole time, and Brady pouts and breaks stuff, but he still keeps taking us. I guess dads are really into ancient toilets?

The only good thing about our trips is that Dad lets me bring my best friend Will Green with us. Will actually loves going because he's pretty much a college professor stuck in a twelve-year-old's body. He spends all his free time reading about history and lecturing us about people and places that I forget about five minutes later. My dad calls him Wikipedia Green. I just call him Wiki.

"I've been giving this a lot of thought, guys, and I've made a decision," I said.

We had stumbled into a quiet, dark section of the store, and it felt uncomfortably silent.

"A hot dog is actually a sandwich. Hear me out. It's got bread on two sides and meat and toppings in the middle."

"Not your sandwich theory again," Wiki said, shaking his head. "Can't we agree to disagree? A hot dog is definitely not a sandwich. For so many reasons!"

"Not just hot dogs either," I continued. "I would consider a burrito a sandwich too. Heck, I would consider an ice cream taco a sandwich. Because the ice cream is sandwiched together between the taco shell."

"That's infuriating!" Wiki snapped. "Just because something's sandwiched between two things doesn't make it a sandwich. And burritos? Where do I even begin?!"

"Guys. Enough. Don't make me break you," Brady said, like she was some action hero. Honestly, my sister could be an action hero. She's in third grade, and her life goal is to become the president's bodyguard, a professional vigilante, or warrior empress of the world. I think she'll probably end up doing all three.

"Shh. Listen."

Purring. Well, it sounded like a six-hundred-pound cat with a deep voice purring, or maybe just burping really slowly. Whatever it was, the sound made my insides shake, and when I looked around, I noticed that Brady and Wiki were also weirded out.

"Um...what exactly is that?" Brady asked, her eyes getting that look that meant she was about to punch something. (She was always about to punch something.)

We hurried toward the sound as Dad studied antique nose-hair trimmers, and there it was. The big oak table that would change everything.

It looked ancient and beat-up but made of good-quality wood (at least that's what Dad said later), and its sides had intricate patterns carved into them. Most importantly, it looked like the kind of table that would make for some truly legendary dinner parties. Dinner parties with muchos sandwiches. I was sold immediately.

I love to cook. More than love—it's hands down my number one all-time favorite thing to do, outranking video games, goat videos, and even the internet. What can I say? Cooking really puts me in the zone and I'm pretty good at it. Plus, it relates to my second-favorite thing: eating.

Brady crept under the table, maybe trying to find a cat. Wiki looked all around the room. Then the purring started again, and immediately we all knew it was coming from the table. A normal-looking, antique dining room table was purring at us. Clearly, we were all going a little loco bananas.

"Is this our new table? Do we have a winner?" Dad asked, walking into the room.

"Dad! You hear it right? That table. Purring. At us. You

hear that, right?" But the purring stopped the second he got there.

Dad raised an eyebrow. "That's the best prank you've got? A purring table?"

"It's not a prank, Papi!" Brady said, shoving him a little. "Give it a second. He'll start again."

"It might sound more like a really slow burp by a sumo wrestler," I added, to be helpful. I burped extra slowly to show him.

Dad looked over at Wiki. "Why do my kids have such a weird sense of humor? I have a great sense of humor."

"Sorry, Mr. Santiago, but I heard it too. And there is no feline in sight."

Dad shrugged his shoulders and walked into the next room, shaking his head. The three of us knew better than to try and convince him, so we did what any normal person would do. We started petting the table. And immediately, the table started purring more loudly.

Brady's usually the muscle in our trio, but she has a soft spot for animals. She started whispering to the table. Wiki and I turned around and pretended she wasn't with us. We kept looking back from the corner of our eyes, but Brady just kept petting the table and whispering to it. She eventually realized that we were standing as far away from her as possible and yelled, "Javi, Wiki—get back here and pet this thing before I kick your butts!" We generally do whatever Brady says (even though she's my little sister), so we got back into it.

Finally, Brady looked at us. "We're getting this table," she said firmly. "Go tell Papi."

"Are you sure you want to buy a piece of furniture that makes us feel delusional?" Wiki asked rubbing his chin nervously.

"We're going to take good care of you, Mr. Table," Brady whispered to it, ignoring Wiki.

Wiki cleared his throat. "I think it has a name. See?" A little plaque on the side of the table was mostly scratched out, but what we could see said "Andu" or maybe "Andy."

"You're going to love living with us, Andy," Brady whispered. And then we went off to find Dad, who was staring lovingly at a one-hundred-year-old chamber pot.

On the way home the three of us sat in the back seat.

"Wow, that guy practically gave that table away. You'd

think it was haunted or something," Dad said from the front seat. "I hope you guys didn't just curse our house—do you know how long it takes to get rid of a curse?"

I knew Dad was mostly joking. I say *mostly* because we're Puerto Rican, and in Puerto Rico most people think that curses are a real thing and that ghost stories are true. But I'm pretty sure Dad only believes in Puerto Rican ghosts, not American ones.

"We just blessed the house, Papi," Brady said. "Just you wait."

"Well, you know what they say." He shrugged. "The light in the front is the one that shines."

Wiki scratched his head and gave me a look. "That doesn't compute."

"Just go with it," I groaned. Dad loves translating Puerto Rican sayings into English because they usually make zero sense. It's his version of a dad joke.

"Let's just pray your mom likes the table when she gets back from Ponce next month," Dad said. "Or back to that kooky store we go." Then he started whistling to himself, and I turned to Wiki and Brady.

"Not a single word about the table to anyone, right?" I whispered.

"It's going to be hard to keep it a secret when Andy starts purring at our friends," Brady said matter-of-factly.

"That was clearly an auditory hallucination produced by that bizarre store," Wiki said, shaking his head. "The table won't purr again."

"Yeah, Brady. Maybe we should pretend this never happened."

Wiki nodded. "That sounds best."

2

The next morning, Brady immediately brought it up.

Wiki rang our doorbell and the three of us headed to school like we always do. It's a short walk because our house is right behind school. Well, the path next to our house leads to a huge football field that's next to a long soccer field that's next to the school. But it's still only a five-minute walk.

"Do you think Andy's going to get lonely while we're at school?" Brady asked as we walked down the path. "Maybe he'd feel better if we put a tablecloth and some plates on him. Or I could set up my dolls on all of his chairs. I told Papi we should've bought a dog. That would have solved it."

"I thought we decided that we wouldn't bring up that strange, impossible piece of furniture," Wiki said.

"It's no biggie, Wiki," I said. "He hasn't purred since we brought him home, so it must've been something weird about that store. Maybe the couches there sneeze and the beds drool."

"Um, Andy purred all night," Brady said, giving us a look. "I snuck down after bed and played tea party with him for hours. It was a nonstop purr-fest."

I groaned. "Seriously? So magic is real, but somehow we've ended up with the dumbest magic of all time! A purring table? We couldn't get a flying carpet or an invisibility cloak or something?"

Wiki shook his head. "I choose to believe that you were merely hallucinating again," he said. "That's the only plausible explanation."

"Oh yeah? Then you should choose to believe that I'm about to punch you in the glasses," Brady growled at him. "Because I am."

I tried to change the subject before she went full Brady on Wiki, but by that point we had taken the path up the hill and we could see our school in the valley below.

No matter how many times you see Finistere, it always makes you forget what you were talking about.

Finistere is an ancient castle plopped into an otherwise normal suburban neighborhood. There are normal houses in front of it, normal basketball courts behind it, a normal playground next to it. Everything around it is exactly what you're used to if you live in the suburbs. Then, smack! Right in the middle of our neighborhood, as if it fell from the sky hundreds of years ago, is Finistere—a full-on, spires-and-everything medieval castle turned into a school. The only thing that's missing is a moat and a dragon.

According to Maryland history, the castle was built in the 1800s by some geeky millionaire who wanted to impress his girlfriend, but when she wouldn't marry him he split. Wiki doesn't buy it, and neither does Dad. "It makes absolutely no sense," Wiki always says. "It's clearly not a modern re-creation. It shouldn't exist here...but I'm glad it does."

I am too. It's by far the awesomest place I've ever visited. The entrance is two enormous doors (I bet it was once a drawbridge) that lead into a big main room where we have assemblies and special events. Then all the rooms along the first floor are high school classrooms. There's a big courtyard in the middle where the high schoolers can hang out after lunch. (They don't call it recess but that's basically what it is.) The second floor is where the principal's office and faculty rooms are. And no one's allowed into the four towers at each corner of the castle, but I hear that there are teachers who actually live up there and never leave the school. Plus, there are rumors of a dungeon under the castle that houses mythical beasts. But that's just nonsense.

If there's one awful thing about Finistere it's that someone thought it'd be rad to tack on a middle school and elementary school and make them boring buildings that look like any other dumb school. I bet it went down like this:

Good Architect: *"How about we build another castle?"*

Bad Architect: *"Nope, let's just build some boring school buildings!"*

Worst Mayor of All Time: *"Ooh, that's a much better idea! Here's the key to the city!"*

So once we get to high school we'll be living life in

style, but for now we have to go to the dumpy middle school and count the days until we get to hang out in the castle. Brady's got it worse—she's in the extra-dumpy elementary school.

Back to the history lesson. The castle was already here when the town was settled, and the millionaire was nowhere to be found. They were going to build the downtown around it, but then there's the woods.

Finistere is bordered by big, dense woods on three sides that seem to go on forever. It feels like the school might be sucked in by the forest at any moment, like the trees are just waiting for the school to look the other way and then they'll swallow it whole. There are completely far-out legends about the woods. Some of the old folks in town say the creepiest things about it—stories of monsters and strange people who lived there and came out at night to cause trouble. No one's seen anything weird for a hundred years, but the woods still spook everyone, and nobody's caught dead venturing into them at night. People warn you about the woods when you're little. "Don't wander too far into the woods" you'll hear grandparents say. "You may never return." When our school has events at night, people pretty much race from their cars into the school, not wanting to linger next to the spooky trees.

But we love the woods. Brady's never been afraid of them, and she's forced us to explore them with her for years. You couldn't pay me enough to walk in them at night, but during the daytime they're pretty magnificent. They also feel like they've been around forever. We sometimes sneak out there during recess because we know no one would ever follow us. And we have some wild forest adventures on weekends. Brady swears she saw a unicorn there once, but she also had an imaginary yeti for a friend back then, so I'm not buying it.

Brady parted ways with Wiki and me when we got into school. She headed to the third-grade hall and we headed to the sixth-grade hall. As usual, we got to science class in the nick of time, and, as usual, we raced onto the ship's deck to get to our desks before the bell rang.

Yep, you read that right. We were halfway through the marine biology unit in life science, the most legendary class in middle school. Real squids in big jars. An octopus in a saltwater aquarium. A ginormous whale skeleton hanging from the ceiling. And class on the reconstructed deck of an old ship. How anyone could cram the deck of a full-sized wooden ship into our classroom was beyond me, but our science teacher could do pretty much anything.

"Everybody aft!" a gruff voice growled. "To your desks at the stern of the ship. Now!" The rest of the class scrambled onto the deck and sat at their desks.

Getting to the best part of sixth grade meant surviving Mr. Scrimshaw. There are plenty of good, nice teachers in the world and way too many bad, mean teachers, but I'd never had a teacher who was both awesome and terrifying. Mr. S looks like a three-hundred-year-old sailor who could still beat you up with one hand tied behind his back. (The scraggly gray hair and gnarly facial scar helps.) He's an incredible storyteller, and he knows more about the ocean that anyone I've ever met, but it also feels like he's one bad kid away from going completely berserk. Everyone loves him and everyone fears him. It's weird. It's great. It's science.

"Now, we begin class the same way we do every day," Scrimshaw said as he walked slowly down each row. *Click. Clack. Click. Clack.* His right leg clicked and clacked mysteriously. As if he wasn't already intimidating enough. "So... Anyone have what I'm looking for? Don't forget, it's extra credit!" As he clicked and clacked down the rows he looked around desperately, hoping someone would raise their hand. Finally Rita lifted hers up shyly. She was holding a newspaper clipping. Mr. S's eyes bulged excitedly as he grabbed the clipping from her hand, reading it as if it were a winning lottery ticket. Then he hung his head and tossed it back on her desk.

"That's the same article Billy brought in last week. Blue whale off the coast of California. Old news." Rita looked sad. "Okay, fine. You get partial credit." Mr. S shook his head. "Anyone else? Any new articles about strange sea creature sightings? Remember, if you find me the right article"—he pointed toward the ship's mast, where he'd nailed up a dirty old coin—"you win the gold."

He started every single class that way. As if that old coin was actual gold.

"All right, class!" he bellowed, reenergized. "Today we'll be studying the fascinating differences between right whales and gray whales. But first I'll pass back yesterday's homework on bowhead whales."

"Bowhead whales are corny!" Buddy Grimes yelled from the back of class. Grimes is our class bully. I'm pretty sure he's half human, half ogre—the dude barely fits in a desk and his hands look like fleshy boulders. I'm also convinced he's either got zero fear or a death wish. He's the only guy I know who's not afraid of Scrimshaw, who practically jumped from the front of the deck to the back, getting in Buddy's face with a maniacal look in his eyes.

"Corny, are they?" he growled. "Maybe I take you to the ocean and introduce you to one up close. Then you can tell me how lame they are. Would you like that, Mr. Grimes? Or are you afraid you'd cry for mommy?" The whole class laughed uproariously. I chuckled too, until Scrimshaw started slapping people's papers onto their desks. "These are facedown because some of you might not like your grades," he muttered.

Grades. The word made me throw up a little bit in my mouth. Two seconds later Scrimshaw slammed my essay down with a D+ scribbled in big red marker and

I practically barfed all over the table. "Better luck next time, bub," he said.

Grades have never been my friend.

3

"**You look like you belong in a Picasso paint-**
ing, from his Blue Period."

"English, Wiki."

"You seem deflated and morose."

"Sad? Is that what you're trying to say?" I grumbled.
"Can't you just use three-letter words instead of spelling-
bee words?"

It was recess, and Wiki and I had snuck into the
woods, walking close enough to the playground that
we'd be able to hear the bell. I was looking down at the
ground like I was staring into the abyss. Wiki studied
me awkwardly.

"Yeesh, you're in a mood."

I looked up at him and heaved a massive sigh. "I got another D in science."

Wiki rubbed his chin. "That's not going to affect your solid C in that class. And given the frequency of Scrimshaw's homework, you could get that up to a B before the year's over."

"Yeah, I'm not that worried about science. It just reminded me about English."

"Ah. Yes. Unfortunately, you're hanging on by a thread in that class. If you don't get an A+ on the next assignment..."

"Don't remind me."

What Wiki was about to say was that if I didn't get an A+ on my next assignment, I was going to have to go to Extra Help English. Then it was a slippery slope—they'd probably switch me out of all of Wiki's classes next year. And that would be the worst thing ever.

"It's not impossible, Javi."

"Oh yeah? Maybe for you. It's like we always say: you're the brains, Brady's the brawn, and I'm the stomach. And school's where I come to get punched in my stomach by tests and homework and occasionally Buddy Grimes."

"Well, I don't know about all that—"

The bell rang, and I snapped out of my funk immediately—we had to hurry back before anyone caught us in the woods.

"English is next. Let's go find out what that essay is," Wiki said as we scrambled out of the forest. Wiki dashed from the edge of the woods to the swings, where other kids were heading in. I was about to follow him when I saw something out of the corner of my eye. I spun around.

Twenty feet behind me there was a shadow peeking out from behind a tree. Something had been watching us. Something that seemed strangely familiar. And unnatural. If I shined a flashlight on it, I bet it would still be a shadow. It was like a living black hole that seemed to whisper, "Hey, kid, haven't had any traumatic nightmares lately? Check me out!"

"I'll catch up in one sec, Wiki," I said. I took a few steps back into the forest to investigate before I realized I was doing the number one thing that kills people in horror movies. So I stopped and listened instead. And somehow that was even worse.

I heard a terrifying movement in the bushes behind the tree. The shadow was running away, except it didn't sound like a human moving through the woods—it sounded like a ginormous monster with twenty legs.

I stood there paralyzed for a full minute.

Then I ran to English class like my life depended on it.

4

"Notebooks out, class," Ms. Vlad **commanded as** she peeked mysteriously out of the closed blinds at the back of the classroom. In seconds we all had our notebooks ready, pencils in hand, and were sitting in perfect silence.

We were super well-behaved in Ms. Vlad's class because our English teacher was obviously a vampire. Sounds loco? It's not like I believed in vampires either— but Ms. Vlad's the worst-disguised vampire of all time. She doesn't even care if her cover's blown.

Let's review the evidence.

- She hates sunlight. The blinds are always shut in our class, and no one's ever seen her walk outside in the daytime. She's the only teacher who never does recess duty.

- She drinks from this old red thermos constantly and is really protective of it, never letting anyone see what's inside. Some kids think it's wine. Wrong. It's definitely one hundred percent blood.

- She's super strict about not letting anyone bring any food into class. (Because, duh—garlic will kill her!)

- Remy dressed up like a vampire hunter for Halloween, and she gave him a death stare all throughout class. I was sure she was going to kill him that day, so I gave him my extra hot dog costume.

The worst part was, only I seemed to accept the truth. Nobody believed me, no matter how much proof I waved in their faces. I was counting the days until Ms. Vlad proved them all wrong, probably in the bloodiest way.

And that's why I'm struggling to get a decent grade. I mean, I've never been great at writing essays, but having Lady Dracula for a teacher doesn't exactly help. I spend most of my time trying to keep a low profile and praying I'm not her first victim. And lately she's seemed extra thirsty for fresh blood.

"Today's homework is very important, class."

Oh boy. Moment of truth. Please be about sandwiches...please be about sandwiches...

"In fact, if you've been at this school for more than one year, you're probably familiar with tonight's assignment."

Oh. Oh wow. This assignment. I knew what she was going to say next.

"It's a question we ask our students every year, and every year we expect all of you to complete it. In fact, it's worth triple an ordinary homework assignment. Doing poorly on this one is not an option." She gave a death stare to the entire class. I heard nervous gulps all around me.

Wiki looked over at me and raised his eyebrows. I smiled.

"I want you to imagine you're hosting a dinner party. If you could invite any three people, living or dead, who would you invite?"

There were a few quiet groans from the class, and someone whispered, "Not again…" but those kids shut up quickly when they remembered whose class they were in.

This was the classic assignment at Finistere. We had it every single year, from kindergarten to twelfth grade. The principal said it was the perfect assignment because it combined writing, history, cooking, and art, but my theory was that the principal was secretly a foodie like me.

Was I the only kid who loved this assignment? It wasn't exactly about sandwiches, but as far as essays go, this one was so up my alley it was ridiculous.

Ms. V sighed. "Okay, I'll elaborate, for those of you who have somehow forgotten about this assignment even though you've done it six times already." She shook her head at us like we were dumb babies. (She was really good at making us feel like dumb babies.) "You can invite any person from history or fiction. For example, would you invite your great-grandpa? Or your favorite character from a book? Or George Washington? Once you've chosen your three people, write about the food you would prepare, the conversations you would have, and the dessert you would serve."

"How long does it have to be?" Ashley blurted out.

"As long as it takes to answer that question well, Ashley," Ms. V said darkly. RIP Ashley.

"I think you forgot the most important part," Dani said with a big smile, trying to be helpful. Dani was a classic teacher's pet. Her sucking up didn't work on Ms. Vlad though, and it was funny to watch her try. Vampires aren't good at making close, emotional connections, and sucking up seems pathetic to them.

"Don't interrupt, Dani," Ms. Vlad growled. "I was just getting to that. The most important part of the assignment. You must take a photo of your table set for these guests, with the actual food and place cards." She scanned the room like she had laser eyes, then added, "It's due Thursday."

There were more groans from the back, but I was smiling so hard my jaw hurt. The Any Three People homework, but worth triple. This might literally be the one essay I could get a decent grade on. I would have to come up with the perfect guest list and the perfect menu, and have Wiki proofread it, but if I did all that... I had a shot.

Everyone wrote the homework down, put their notebooks away, and then read in silence for thirty minutes, while Ms. V studied each of our necks from her desk, drinking from her thermos. Weird, right? I'm telling you, we are TERRIFIED of Ms. V.

When the bell rang, I took a deep breath. An A+ essay for Lady Dracula. Well, here goes nothing.

5

"So, who will you invite?" I asked Wiki as we walked to his aunt's house that afternoon.

Wiki rubbed his chin as he thought. "It's a difficult question. At this point we've done this assignment six times, so we've invited eighteen people total. I have at least three hundred more I'd like to invite, but I imagine our classmates are running out of options."

"Yeah, I bet they repeat dinner guests. I think I've invited Benjamin Franklin three times by now."

"Indeed. Most people are probably going to pick Abraham Lincoln, Albert Einstein, and Amelia Earhart."

"No, more like someone from that band Boi Squad."

"Hmm, yes," he said, shuddering. "Now, who to invite... I suppose it depends on the conversation you want to have at dinner. I would choose some of history's lesser-known heroes. The ones we don't learn about in class. I'm not that curious about most presidents or old baseball players. Give me Nikolai Tesla, Ada Lovelace, or Hattori Hanzō any day."

Sometimes I think Wiki was raised by statues in a museum.

"That homework again?" Brady grumbled. "We did ours last month."

"Who'd you invite?" I asked her.

She looked at me very seriously and nodded as she said, "Hammy."

"Hammy, our old hamster?" I shook my head and Wiki laughed. Brady's face went red. (With anger of course, not embarrassment. Never embarrassment.)

"What's so funny? I miss Hammy, and I wanted to know how she's doing. Plus, she just eats lettuce, so she'd be easy to cook dinner for. Oh, and she can read minds, so she can tell me why Trevor keeps giving me all these weird looks during class."

"I can tell you that." Wiki laughed. "It's because he likes you."

"Ew," she spit out. "I trust Hammy's opinion more than yours."

I threw my hands up in the air. Neither of them was any help. And Wiki was right. I didn't want to write about George Washington or Thomas Edison like everyone else in class. I was sure Ms. Vlad would give extra points for originality. But where would I begin to look for the right person? Would Google have any results for "awesome-but-not-quite-famous people from history?" Doubt it. And I wasn't about to flip through our old encyclopedias.

"Maybe I'll just ask Aunt Nancy for her advice," I sighed as we walked across her front lawn. Aunt Nancy was Wiki's favorite aunt, and one of the most mysterious and generally awesome grown-ups I'd ever met. Even Wiki couldn't guess her age, and he knew surprisingly little about her past. Wiki's parents worked late, so he basically lived with her during the week. Her house was two blocks away from ours, and I loved hanging out there after school.

"Hi, Aunt Nancy," Wiki called out as we walked into her dark house. It was always pretty dark in there. We headed into her living room and plopped our bags on the floor.

There were a few things about Aunt Nancy's house that were either extremely creepy or extremely cool, depending on your love of weirdness. For one, silk tapestries were hung between every room and across every doorway. They were gorgeous—colorful and mesmerizing—but they were everywhere. Walking through her house, you were constantly using your arms to swim through the tapestries that were always in your way. But the even stranger thing was that Aunt Nancy decorated her ceilings as if they were walls. The ceiling in every room had paintings, mirrors, and, in a few cases, even windows. When you asked her about it, she just kind of shrugged it off and said that people decorated things differently where she was from. Wiki's family is originally from Haiti, which is right next to Puerto Rico, so I didn't buy it. People would think my abuela was bizarre if she started nailing family photos to the ceiling.

"Aunt Nancy?" Wiki called again, lifting the tapestries between the living room and the kitchen. The smell of dinner wafted in. I lifted my nose into the air to catch every bit of the aroma, and it made me feel like I was floating. Aunt Nancy was the best cook I'd ever met. She was the only person I knew who combined Caribbean cuisine with soul food, and that fusion was so good it felt like it actually fed your soul. Today it smelled like corn bread, fried okra, and something made of sweet potatoes. I crossed my fingers that she'd let me try a little bit.

"Three sets of feet going pitter-patter pitter-patter," she called out from upstairs. "Is that Brady and the magnificent Javier?" (We're both chefs, so we have a special bond.) She made her way down the stairs and smiled as she walked into the living room. Her smile was always a little wicked, and it might have freaked you out a little bit if you didn't know her. "And what's my little trio of terror up to today?" she asked as she sat on the couch and picked up her knitting.

I explained our homework assignment and how badly I needed to ace it.

"So, if you could invite any three people in the history of the world to dinner, who would it be?" I finally asked.

"Ah, this question. This is the classic question. A question that gets asked a lot in our town. A question that gets people in trouble." She looked up at her ceiling at a framed drawing of some trees, staring into it like she was remembering something that happened long ago.

"Ahem," I said as politely as I could.

"Well, the guests are the wrong place to start," she continued, looking at me again. "The real question is, what's the purpose of the meal? You can cook to feed and to entertain, but some people cook to poison, to overthrow a king, to start a revolution. Some cook to win the hand of their beloved, some cook to bring a family or a kingdom together or tear them apart. And there are those of us," she said turning to me and smiling mischievously, "who have cooked for all those reasons. So what is the purpose of this meal, Javier?"

I stopped to try to think of a good answer that would impress her.

"To let people from olden times try sandwiches?"

Wow, Javi. Really impressive...yeesh.

She nodded slowly, then went on. "Well, what happens after the dinner? Sure, you can invite presidents and kings, artists and assassins, inventors and dancers, but how long will they stay?"

"It's just dinner, Aunt Nancy," Wiki said. "As if we were having a dinner party. The guests arrive, eat, and go back to their homes."

"But it sounds like these guests don't have a home. At least not here. A home is more than a place—it's also a time. And right now it is your time. Not theirs."

Aunt Nancy was really overthinking this. "You know what, I think we're good. Thanks for helping, Aunt Nancy," I said. Better to move on to another subject. "Could I try some of that corn bread?"

"Why, you most certainly can!" she said excitedly as she hopped over to the kitchen. "Let's see if you figure out the secret ingredient this time!" I was really good at figuring out secret ingredients.

She came over with a big piece of corn bread for each of us. She gave one to Brady, to Wiki, and then, as she gave me a piece, she paused and looked me in the eye.

"Just be careful who you invite to dinner, Javi. There are good guests and bad guests."

"It's just homework, Aunt Nancy."

"Of course it is," she said, looking at me intently. "Of course it is."

"Cumin," I said, biting into her amazing corn bread. It was definitely cumin.

"Correct!" she said, clapping once.

She walked back into the kitchen to get herself a piece of corn bread. Wiki whispered, "Hey, Javi, you're going to set up the meal for the photos tonight, right? Like you always do?" I nodded. "If I give you a bunch of options for guests, will you help me fix up a good dinner and take some pictures of it?"

"That sounds like the best trade of all time. Done and done."

"All right, I'll be over after dinner. Make those legendary tostones."

6

Tostones (pronounced toast-tone-ness) are a Puerto Rican classic and my specialty. You take a plantain—basically a big banana that tastes gross raw but delicious cooked—cut it up, smash it, fry it twice, then dip it in garlic and oil. There's no better food in the world, I guarantee it. I bet we could achieve world peace if all the world leaders got together and ate tostones. Who could go to war after experiencing that magical blend of garlic and fried banana in their mouth?

I was finishing up my third batch of tostones, and the smell was already wafting through the entire house. I was in my happy place. Brady kept running through the kitchen, swiping tostones as I finished each batch. I shouted at Dad to tell her to stop, and she gave me a little punch in the gut. That shut me right up. Then the doorbell rang, and Wiki walked in.

"DO I SMELL TOSTONES?!" he yelled as he walked in.

Dad wasn't too thrilled with the idea of me cooking a second dinner, especially one that would go to waste, so he just let me make a bunch of tostones and set the table. I made it look a little more legit by taking some of our fruit and bread and placing them in a nice decorative little basket in the center of the table. And then I did my pièce de résistance—what sets me apart from all the amateur dinner party enthusiasts—napkins folded like swans. It never fails to get an *ooh* and an *aah* from anyone who sees it.

"Ooh. Aah." Wiki walked around the table looking impressed, especially at the swans.

I leaned on Andy and he purred. Wiki cupped his ears, scrunched his eyes closed, and repeated, "I didn't hear that. I didn't hear that. I didn't hear that."

I chuckled. "Yeah, he's still doing that. Hey, Andy, any chance you can transform into a royal table—the kind a king would have in his palace?"

Wiki immediately jumped back, his hands in front of his face. Andy stopped purring, so I shrugged.

"It was worth a try. Hey, Andy, if you have any tricks that might get me an A+ on this assignment, go nuts."

Andy purred, and Wiki shook his head, his eyes wide. "Don't listen to him, Andy. We'll be fine without any tricks, thank you very much." He glared at me.

I rolled my eyes. "Okay, friendo, you have one deluxe table and dinner courtesy of Chez Javi. Now how about you rustle up some guest ideas for me?"

"Absolutely, just stop involving Andy. So, what general ideas do you have?"

I looked at him blankly for a second. "Um...none. Nothing."

"Don't be lazy, Javi. You're the one who actually loves throwing dinner parties, not me. What makes for a good dinner party?"

"Hmm... Fair question. I've never really broken it down like that before. I guess good conversation, good music, and good food."

"Perfect. Let's start with music. What musician should we invite?"

"Well, I guess if it's for school it'd better be Mozart. Who else, right?"

Wiki shook his head. "Mozart?! As if there were only one great classical musician in all of history! Shame on you, Javi. Let's broaden your horizons a bit, shall we? Why not pick someone who makes great dinner party music. Really knock-you-off-your-feet beautiful music. The kind of music that regularly brings people to tears."

"Boi Squad?" Brady said from under the table where she was doing her homework. Ever since Andy moved in, she was always hanging out close to him.

"Claude Debussy. One of the most influential composers of the last century. He could melt our hearts on that old piano you've got in the corner, if we could convince him to play it."

"Yeah, but I don't know anything about the guy. I know everyone picks Mozart, but at least I know some of his music and I could write about him."

Wiki groaned. "Well, how can we make him more interesting? Maybe pick Mozart as a child. By the time he was our age, Wolfgang Amadeus Mozart had composed his first symphony and was playing for royalty around Europe."

"Kid Mozart! Done. Good call—that's got to be worth an A. Okay, that's the music, and I've taken care of the food, so all we need is some good conversation."

"Well, what do you want to talk about? What's the conversation you want to have?"

I looked at him blankly. "I don't know. Who's interesting?"

Wiki laughed. "Well, my father and I agree that Theodore Roosevelt and Ida Wells are two of the most interesting people in history, although I think ascribing that title to anyone would be highly controversial. But maybe you should choose someone who...shares a specific interest of yours."

"Are you saying they're too smart for me?" I gave him a look and he winced.

"No, that's not what I meant! Not at all. Just that their interests might not overlap with yours."

"Okay, okay, let me see... Well, what do I like? I used to be pretty into dinosaurs... I went through that monsters-with-squid-heads phase last year... Oh, I know. Duh. Sandwiches!"

"Sandwiches? Are you serious?"

"Yeah, I want to talk to the inventor of the sandwich. Maybe he can settle our sandwich debate once and for all. Any idea who that is?"

"John Montagu, the fourth Earl of Sandwich."

"That's seriously his name? The Earl of Sandwich? Yeah, that's definitely a guy I want at my dinner party!"

Wiki rolled his eyes. "Out of literally every human in history, you're inviting the Earl of Sandwich to your dinner party. Why are we friends? Remind me."

"Ha! You're just scared he'll side with me—you'll have to call hot dogs sandwiches from now on!"

"Never," Wiki said through gritted teeth.

"Okay, I need one last person who's just purely a kiss-up choice. Someone who sounds very teacherly and academic. Like Billy A++ or Mary WowDoILoveTeachers or something."

"Interesting strategy. Give me a moment." Wiki looked toward the ceiling and started tracing invisible lines in the air with his finger, which is usually how I know he's doing deep thinking. His eyes went wide and then he started laughing. "Teach! Edward Teach! How perfect is that?"

I smiled and nodded. "Almost too perfect. Wow. Is he famous?"

Wiki nodded quickly. "Incredibly famous. Oh yeah. Big-time."

"What is he—a famous explorer?"

He chuckled again. "Yeah, something like that."

"What's so funny?" I asked, giving him a suspicious look. I know better than to trust Wiki when he laughs.

"Nothing—nothing at all. It's just so perfect."

"I don't know," I said. "I should probably pick someone I know really well. Otherwise, I'll have to do all this research on top of writing the essay and then—"

"One hour till bed, Javi!" Dad called from his room.

"Okay, forget it. Mr. Teach it is. Let's do this!"

7

Andy was looking really good by the time I borrowed Dad's phone to take some pics. Besides the killer decorations, the delicious spread, and the fancy plates (I convinced Dad to let me use the good china since we weren't actually eating from it), I printed out place cards using our thick printer paper and a swirly old font that gave it that extra touch of class. I must say, "John Montagu, Fourth Earl of Sandwich" looked extremely awesome printed out in that font. I wondered who I would have to convince to take up that title. "Javier Santiago, three-hundredth Earl of Sandwich" had a pretty nice ring to it. And I bet Montagu's best creation couldn't touch my next-level sandos.

"Brady, could you evacuate the premises while we complete this photo shoot?" Wiki asked, since Brady still hadn't left her post under Andy. "I feel that you might be a little out of place in these photos." For once, Brady didn't get angry and instead jumped up and grabbed a tostone as she circled the table for a better look.

"Looking good, gents. Kind of stinks that it's just pretend and we can't have this dinner."

"Trust me, this would be an extremely awkward dinner. Javi picked a very unusual trio, to put it mildly. You wouldn't catch me dead eating dinner with the Earl of Sandwich and Edward Teach."

"Who's Edward Teach?" she asked innocently. Out of the corner of my eye I saw Wiki wink and put his finger to his lips.

"Wiki, if you're playing a prank on me after I spent an hour making these glorious origami napkin swans..." I gave him one of my signature glares. Wiki hates my glares.

And then Andy began to shake.

For a second I thought Andy was laughing at Wiki's prank, but then all I could think about was Dad storming into the dining room and wondering why our new dining room table was possessed.

Brady leapt over to Andy and started petting him. "What's wrong, Andy? Don't worry. They weren't really fighting. Everything's okay. Shhh."

But Andy kept shaking, even more violently now.

"He's going to shake the china onto the floor, and Dad is going to murder us!" I shouted. "Everybody, grab the china!"

Wiki and I practically jumped on the table and were about to grab the glasses and plates when Brady leapt in front of us, making a stop sign with one hand and shushing us with the other one. "Listen! Andy's not trying to sabotage your homework. Do you hear that? I think he's trying to show us something."

At first all I heard was the rumbling of plates and glasses, and I almost pushed past Brady to pick up the china anyway, but I realized she had a point. There was a really high-pitched metallic sound that was coming from inside the table. She moved the chairs to the side and dove under Andy, her back on the floor as she explored the underside of the table like a mechanic checking a car. Wiki and I watched her, wondering if she was right. Her hands started feeling around under the center of the table when she yelped.

"There's something here! It's...it's a secret compartment!"

Wiki and I both scuttled over to see, knocking our heads together in the process.

"Quit crowding me, guys! Let me get this thing open. It's a teeny little latch. I bet no one's ever noticed it before. Here it goes... Now, I just slide this little thing to the side and... Hey! Whoa!"

Something shiny dropped onto Brady's stomach and she quickly swiped it and rolled out from under Andy, exploring her new treasure.

It was a silver bell. And it looked like it had never been touched before. Without thinking, Wiki and I both grabbed for it.

"Hey, stop! Let me take a closer look." Brady easily pushed us away with one hand as she studied the bell with the other. "Wow, there's something written on it."

"Perhaps you should let someone familiar with Latin

take a look, as I imagine the arcane words might be impossible for you to understand."

"Um, if it's not in English, it's pretty obvious. It's just three words." As she spoke the words, she let Wiki and I get close enough to it that we could read the inscription.

INVITER
ET
DESINVITER

Wiki's brow furrowed. "French? Invite and disinvite." His finger traced an invisible pattern in the air as he worked something out in his head.

"What do you think it means?" I asked.

"Only one way to find out," Brady said, raising the bell above her head. I could hear Wiki screaming "Noooooo" as Brady shook it.

Andy started purring louder than ever. Louder. Louder. A deafening purr...

Then everything got really weird.

8

It wasn't exactly an explosion—more like an epic burst of light that seemed to come from Andy. We threw our hands up over our eyes and all took a few steps back, completely blinded for a second.

Before we could really tell what was going on in front of us, we heard them. There were definitely other people in the room with us who hadn't been there a second ago. And we smelled them. It might have been the worst stench I've ever experienced in my life. Despite being a mix of shocked, surprised, and horrified, we couldn't help but pinch our noses immediately—it smelled like someone had taken a long, hot bath in raw sewage.

"Well isn't this a rather odd establishment for a

dinner fete of this caliber?" a stodgy voice with a strong British accent stated. "I thought this would be a dinner party for the ages."

"Feels fancy enough to me," growled another voice—a very rough, scratchy one.

"Something smells delicious!" said a high-pitched kid's voice.

When my eyes finally adjusted, I realized I wasn't dreaming. There were three complete strangers sitting at our table. And they seemed pretty hungry.

One of them was wearing fancy clothes and jewelry and seemed like the kind of royalty that belonged in a castle with a squire. Another was a kid our age wearing a white wig and some really uncomfortable clothes from what looked like hundreds of years ago.

But the third guy was the stuff of nightmares. He was tall and imposing, and his eyes had this devilish look that chilled me to the bone. He was dressed in black and had a long, dark beard that went up all the way to his eyes and down to his chest. It was knotted and tangled like brambles. Also, I could swear that there were little tufts of smoke rising up from his beard. Had it been on fire before?! Oh, and he smelled exactly like a sewer.

He picked up a fork and pointed it directly at Brady, Wiki, and me. "Am I right in assuming that you three are our hosts?"

This might have been the most awkward moment in my life. Wiki and I stared in terror. The guests stared back in confusion. Brady saved the day, as usual. She didn't even miss a beat.

"Welcome to Casa de Brady, home of fine dining! Make yourselves comfortable and we'll start serving you. I'm Brady, and these are my associates, Javi and Wiki."

"Hobby and Kiwi, did you say? By the queen, those aren't real, respectable names. Give us your real names at once, children," said the royal-looking guy. I could already tell he was going to be a royal pain in the butt.

"Ahem, m-m-my name is William, sir, and this is Javier," said Wiki in a nervous but overly formal voice. "An honor to meet you, y-y-your highness."

"Highness?" the stinky-sewer guy burped. "Who might you be?" he said as he poked a finger at the royal pain.

"Mind your manners, peasant—you're speaking to John Montagu, Fourth Earl of Sandwich, also known as Viscount Hinchingbrooke and Baron Montagu of Saint Neots."

The bearded nightmare's eyes got really narrow and it looked like a fight was brewing. Thankfully the kid saved the day.

"A pleasure to meet all of you," the little boy said kindly, waving and kicking his feet merrily under the table. "I am Wolfgang Amadeus. This meal looks quite exceptional. Not as fancy as my dinner with the princess, but in truth it smells even better."

"So if you're the Earl of Sandwich, and if you're Mozart..." Brady began asking.

"Don't!" Wiki whispered loudly to her. "You don't want to know. Trust me. You don't want to ask that question."

The dirty, drenched dude heard Wiki and laughed. "It appears," he said darkly, "that only one of you realizes who you invited to dinner." He looked slowly at each of us, a wicked smile growing on his face. "Nobody else?" The room got perfectly silent and Wiki gulped so hard

I could swear that it made the floor shake. He started backing away toward the door, too afraid to turn from the dinner guest.

Then, in a flash, the guest pulled something thin and shiny from his pocket and flung it toward Wiki. Before anyone could scream, we heard a thud. Wiki made a noise like he'd been hit, and everyone gasped. But then he opened his eyes and looked over at his hand. His right sleeve was pinned to the front door by a big, fat dagger.

"It's rude for a host to leave his own dinner party," Beardo chuckled. "Now tell your friends who you invited to dinner, and then let's all sit down and have ourselves a nice little meal."

Wiki stuttered for a good minute before he could get a word out. "M-m-m-m-meet Edward Teach. B-b-b-better known as...Blackbeard."

The Earl of Sandwich dropped his fork, and his eyes went wide. I stared in horror. Brady turned to me and yelled, "You invited Blackbeard the pirate to the dinner party?!"

"Wiki!" I shrieked. "This was your stupid prank! Now look what you've done!"

But I couldn't feel too angry at Wiki. His eyes were the size of floodlights, and he was visibly trembling.

"Can somebody pass the bread, please?" Kid Mozart asked sweetly. "I'm starving."

9

It was a pretty memorable dinner. Not exactly in a good way. The Earl of Sandwich was definitely a royal pain in the butt, and he kept asking us to fetch him food we didn't have—stuff that nobody eats these days, like roast puffin, quiche lorraine, and mock turtle soup. When we told him we didn't have any of it, he got really snooty. He also kept suggesting we play elaborate card games I'd never heard of and pouting when we said no. All in all, I couldn't believe he was the guy who invented the greatest food of all time.

Kid Mozart was supremely awesome, though. He was super polite but also told a lot of funny jokes and great stories about different royal palaces around Europe that he had visited. I've gotta say, he's a couple of years younger than me and he's already hung out with a bunch of kings and queens and is basically a celebrity in Europe—what have I done with my life so far? I can barely even play "Three Blind Mice"!

Blackbeard was quiet for most of the dinner. He just looked around the table mysteriously and stole glances at the other rooms in the house. He was definitely up to no good, and I could tell that Wiki noticed too. Wiki was still trembling a little bit and stuttering throughout the meal. Honestly, if it hadn't been for Kid Mozart, it might have been one of the worst dinners of all time.

In an attempt to save the night, I hopped into the kitchen for a few minutes and put together one of my patented Javi Specialty Sandwiches—a double-decker beauty with Puerto Rican ingredients on one layer and American ingredients on the other: the Spanglish Sandwich!

We were just finishing up the meal when I brought it out on a covered-up plate. I stood next to the earl, and like a magician pulling a rabbit out of a hat, whisked the cover off, revealing my glorious Spanglo Sando.

"Ta-da! It's your royal invention, except way better. This one won third place in a school contest."

The earl arched one eyebrow and gave me a nasty look. "What is this monstrosity?"

"Wait," I said, stunned. "You don't even know what a sandwich is? You mean I literally invited you here for nothing?!"

The earl made a face at me. "I hope you don't expect me to eat this ridiculous mess of bread and the queen knows what else. Begone, shoo!"

When it comes to bullies, Brady acts way more like a big sister than a little one. She hates when people are mean to me (which is a pretty constant thing), and I could see her rage flaring. She stomped over to the earl and put her face so close to his that their noses were practically touching. "Listen here, Buster. You're going to eat the food Javi made you, or else. He just made a whole mess in the kitchen building you this award-winning sandwich, and now I'm going to watch you eat it. Bite. By. Bite. Now chew."

Blackbeard laughed. "I like this girl! You ever considered piracy? You'd be a fierce one!"

Brady blushed and curtsied.

Then Blackbeard turned to the earl. "I agree with the girl. Eat that sandwich or I'm gonna introduce you to Bessie." He then pulled another, bigger dagger out of his boot, placed it gently on the table, and tapped on it twice. "Bessie would love to get to know you."

The earl silently ate the sandwich, the whole time staring wide-eyed at the dagger on the other side of the table. Brady was beaming. Blackbeard was smiling wickedly. Everyone else seemed to be embarrassed by the whole situation and was looking awkwardly at other things in the room.

"The story goes," Wiki whispered to me, "that the earl was so obsessed with gambling, that once he started playing he never wanted to leave his card table. Since eating fork-and-knife foods while playing cards was too awkward, he invented a food he could eat with his hands. That's how the sandwich was born. I guess he hasn't done it yet."

I nodded sadly. I was hoping the sandwich had been invented in the middle of a sword fight or castle siege and used as a delicious weapon. Catapults filled with sandwiches—now *that* was an origin story.

"Well, that's enough entertainment for one evening." Blackbeard chuckled, rising out of his seat and exploring our living room, picking up objects and studying them as we stared in terror. He made his way to our bookshelf and started scanning titles.

"Blackbeard can read?" the earl whispered to himself.

"Compared to you, I'm a scholar," the pirate mumbled gruffly, casually tapping on Bessie as he picked up a book about pirates. The earl gulped and probably peed his pants.

"Three chapters on old Edward Teach!" Blackbeard smiled, flipping through the book. "Wait 'til I tell Stede Bonnet and the chaps about this."

He read the book, and we all stared at him in stunned silence. I'd been afraid to make eye contact with him before, so now I was finally taking a good look at him. Blackbeard would probably haunt my dreams forever. He was even more towering than I'd first realized, and his beard seemed like a separate monster living on his face, even more evil than he was. Between the blood-shot eyes and the tufts of smoke, Blackbeard seemed more like a demon than a man. And here he was reading a book in our living room like it was the most normal thing in the world.

"What's this?" Blackbeard muttered. "This is impossible." He kept reading, his demon eyes getting wider and angrier. "Robert Maynard? Who?" He read faster now, flipping page after page, his anger rising with each flip. "What?!" He slammed the book closed, threw it to the floor, and looked up at us. For a split second it looked like he was going to pull out his dagger and murder us, but then he remembered where he was, and his dark scowl turned into a creepy smile. "Excuse me," he said, sitting back down at the table.

Creepy silence.

"I see you have a piano," Kid Mozart said after clearing his throat, cutting through the awkwardness and saving the day yet again. "Allow me to play you a few songs."

He jumped out of his seat and skipped over to the piano. When he saw it up close, he gasped loudly. "This is the most incredible piano I have ever seen!" He shyly pushed down on a few keys and then listened intently at the sound. "The sound is angelic. More beautiful than the pianos in the courts of Vienna and Paris. Is this the greatest piano in the world?".

I scratched my head, unsure how to answer him because I really didn't want to let him down.

"Ha! We got that piece of junk in a garage sale for free," Brady said. Yep, that's what I didn't want to tell him.

"Piece of junk? You call this exquisite miracle a piece of junk? Tell me this sounds like the music a piece of junk produces." With that Kid Mozart sat down, cracked his knuckles above his head, and proceeded to play the most beautiful music I'd ever heard in my life. It looked impossible to play—his hands flew across the keys so quickly I was pretty sure his arms were made of rubber, and his fingers played the notes so perfectly I wondered if he was secretly a robot. (MozartBot! I liked the ring of that.)

Everyone fell under Kid Mozart's spell. His music had us completely hypnotized. Nobody spoke or even seemed to breathe the entire time he played. Out of the corner of my eye, I saw Blackbeard cry a single tear. Little Wolfgang played and played, song after song after song, but nobody wanted him to stop. It didn't matter if you were into rock music or hip-hop or jazz, or even if you hated classical music—it was the best music you'd ever heard.

When he finally stopped playing, nobody spoke for a long time. We all stared at the floor, stunned. The first person to say anything was the earl, and he just started crying loudly. "I'm so bloody sorry for my rudeness!" he sobbed. "You're perfectly wonderful hosts, the food has been delicious, the music divine, and that breaded dish you gave me was quite exquisite too. Oh, I'm nothing but a royal rudesby, a good-for-nothing royal rudesby. I repent! I repent! When I return to my home I'll renounce gambling and live a life of virtue and generosity!" Then he put his face in his hands and sobbed even more loudly. We all looked at the floor and pretended we couldn't hear him. This guy was the Earl of Awkwardness!

"Well, my fine new friends, this was a perfectly lovely evening, and I hope we're able to dine again soon. I will begin composing a new song to play on your magnificent piano. I do grow a bit tired, and Papa will worry about me if I'm not home soon." Mozart yawned.

"We can get you home in a jiffy!" Brady jumped up out of her daze and gave Kid Mozart a big hug. "I used to hate taking piano lessons, but now all I want to do is play like you do."

Kid Mozart laughed. "That will be no problem if you practice eight to ten hours a day, seven days a week!"

Brady made a face like she'd just eaten poop. "Well, I want to play piano better than I do, anyway. Maybe not as good as you." She then took a look at the bell. "Okay, have a seat at the table. When I ring this thing, I bet you'll be home in no time."

Mozart hugged Wiki and me warmly before he took a seat. What a great guy. I hugged him back. Wiki was still too in shock to do anything but look sick. You couldn't blame him—he almost got stabbed by a pirate and then two minutes later was listening to the most beautiful music in the world. It was a lot to take in!

The earl waved goodbye sadly but didn't get up from his seat. Instead he blew his nose really hard into one of our nice napkins and then put it on the table. Ew. Thanks again, Earl.

Blackbeard pointed at Brady. "Hope you'll join my

crew one day, milady. You would be one of the fiercest pirates on the sea. Maybe one day I'd kill my first mate and make you second-in-command. In the meantime, learn to tie some ship knots and practice raiding merchant vessels." Brady nodded proudly. Blackbeard ignored Wiki and me completely. I wasn't sad about it.

Brady then petted the table. "Okay, Andy, time to send our new friends home." She held the bell over her head and rang it loudly. A flash of lightning blinded us all again, and there was silence in the room. I rubbed my eyes for a few seconds, waiting to open them again and pretend that the whole dinner party was a dream. Ah, back to good old normal life.

Instead, I heard Wiki scream, "Wait, where are you going? You can't—ow!"

Then there was a big thud followed by an even bigger thud, and our front door slammed.

10

First I saw a lump on the floor. Then I realized that lump was Wiki. Brady and I ran over to him and noticed that he wasn't moving. "Wiki! Wake up! What happened?" I shook him and shook him, but he just lay there. "Oh no—Wiki is dead! Wikiiiiiiiii!"

Brady rolled her eyes. "Put your finger under his nostrils, dummy—he's still breathing. He just got knocked out."

I breathed a massive sigh of relief. And then I got worried again. "Well, we need to figure something out to make sure he doesn't die! Maybe he's just knocked out for now, but... Brady, get a doctor!" I lifted Wiki's head onto my lap, hoping his life wasn't fading away. "Stay with us Wiki! Don't die—you'd be a super-annoying ghost!"

Brady's eye roll was even bigger this time. "Must I do everything, Javi?" She slapped Wiki, and a muffled groan came from his mouth.

"Sorry, Wiki." Brady shrugged. "Javi thought you were dead."

Wiki's eyes gradually started opening, and he slowly turned his head from side to side. "Wiki lives!" I yelled, dropping his head on the floor in my excitement.

"Ow! Please don't make me pass out again," he said, rubbing his head. He shot up into a sitting position. "Did you catch him? He didn't get away, did he? Please tell me he didn't get away."

Brady and I looked at him blankly. "What are you talking about?" I asked. Then I remembered the noise. "Oh yeah, you were saying something when the light flashed, and then we heard a few thuds and maybe the door slamming." As I said it, I realized what happened.

"Blackbeard!" Wiki whispered in horror. "He jumped out of the chair right before you rang the bell and made a run for the door. I covered my eyes for the flash, so I wasn't blinded. Then I stupidly got in his way, but he just knocked me out with the butt of his dagger and left."

"There's a real-life pirate in our world now?" Brady asked quietly. She let out a low, sad whistle. "Well, that's not good."

"Not just a pirate," Wiki said, breathing harder and louder, his eyes getting a wild look. "Most historians consider Blackbeard the most dangerous pirate in history. And one of the most feared people in all of history. The damage he could do here...it's frightening. It's...it's..." Wiki looked like he was about to explode.

"Chill, Wiki," Brady said.

"Chill? Chill?!" Wiki looked at her in disbelief. "One of the most brilliant, powerful villains in all of history is loose in our world! In our neighborhood! And it's entirely my fault!"

He looked at back and forth at Brady and me a hundred times, his brain going a trillion miles an hour. Finally he stopped, looked me in the eyes, and nodded. "I have a lot to figure out. Or our lives are in danger. Not just ours. Everyone's." He was quiet for a second, then nodded again. "Bye."

Wiki bolted out the door and scrambled toward his house, as fast as anyone would run if there was a deadly pirate loose in their neighborhood. I went to close the door behind him and watched him sprint down the street, into the night.

Then something familiar caught my eye. On the other side of the street, someone who had been watching our house slid into the darkness and disappeared. But it wasn't the pirate. It was the shadow.

The shadow from the woods. The one I saw at recess.

"Um, Brady? Can you come here for a—" But I couldn't finish my sentence because Dad came out of his room and stumbled into the kitchen for a drink of water. Then he noticed the lights on everywhere.

"Javi? Brady? Why are you guys up? It's three in the morning," he said groggily. "And it smells like a... sewer?"

"Run!" said Brady, and we scrambled to our rooms, to the weirdest nightmares ever.

11

The next morning Wiki didn't walk to school with us, answer his phone, or let us know that he was even alive. A few teachers mentioned that he was home sick, so we knew he wasn't dead, but I doubted he had a cold or the flu. I wondered if he was going to come back to school at all. Brady and I whispered back and forth about our dinner party as we walked to Finistere, but we weren't sure what to do next. All I could do was check the news online during library class and hope that there was no mention of a pirate wreaking havoc on our town. So far so good, but I knew it was only a matter of time before things went south.

Maybe I was desperate to process everything that had

happened or maybe I just had a lot of nervous energy, but all through breakfast and library class I scrawled out every last detail of our dinner party, all the way up to the Blackbeard incident. English class was third period, and I turned in my secretly nonfiction essay feeling weirdly proud. I'd even printed out pics from Dad's phone before heading to school. I was pretty worried that Ms. Vlad would give me an F because it was such an unbelievable story, but the opposite happened.

She handed the essay back at the end of class and gave me the most intense look. It wasn't a murderous look, exactly. More like the look you give someone who's about to jump out of a plane. First I noticed that she gave me back a photocopy of my essay with the pictures missing. Weird. Then I looked at the essay itself. A++. 110%.

I did it! I was ecstatic. I felt like a million bucks. I pumped my fist in the air and was about to let out a big "Yessssss!" when I remembered that there was still a pirate on the loose in our town and staying in Wiki's English class wouldn't matter much if we were both dead. Thanks a lot, Blackbeard, for ruining my moment. At least Dad would be super jazzed when I told him.

Wiki showed up in the middle of fifth period. He didn't say a word to me, and he looked awful. I was pretty sure he hadn't slept since I last saw him, and I was guessing he hadn't eaten much either. His eyes were red, and he kept them focused on the floor at all times. I tried talking to him between classes, but he just nodded glumly and mumbled answers to my questions so quietly I could barely hear him.

He sat on a swing at recess, far away from the other kids, and he didn't seem super excited when Brady and I joined him. Usually I hate it when Brady tries to hang out with us at recess, but this time I was just fine with it. We had a lot to talk about. For a long time we just stared at Wiki, and he stared firmly at the ground. I wasn't really sure where to begin.

"Hey, I got an A++ on that essay, Wiki. Looks like we'll stay in the same English class after all," I said, smiling weakly.

Wiki nodded and gave me an unenthusiastic thumbs-up without making eye contact.

Brady threw a stick at Wiki.

"Wiki, stop being a jerk. We need to make a plan,

and being Glummy McGlummerson isn't going to solve anything. Quit feeling sorry for yourself already."

That woke him up. He glared at Brady. "We've unleashed a monster on the world, and it's all my fault."

Brady didn't miss a beat. "Well, get over it, mister. You're not solving anything slumped over in a swing like that."

I tried to soften Brady's sting. "There are a few things we should probably debrief on, Wiki."

Wiki nodded and we ventured into the woods where we wouldn't be overheard. "I've been doing a lot of thinking between vomiting sessions," he admitted.

"Thinking? Who would've guessed?" Brady said, trying to make a joke. Bad timing, Brady. Wiki just glared at her.

"First, we need to agree not to use Andy again," Wiki said firmly. "Who knows who else we could unleash on the world, even with our best intentions."

"Are you kidding?" Brady said, throwing her hands up. "That's how we defeat Blackbeard! Do you think the three of us can take on that skunky pirate alone? I mean, maybe me... But still. I'd rather invite a bunch of knights to clobber him and be done with it."

Wiki shook his head even more firmly. "Trust me. Something will go wrong. Look, let's at least agree not to use Andy for the next few days, until we find out what happened to Blackbeard."

Brady crossed her arms and nodded gruffly.

"Most importantly," Wiki continued, "where's the bell?"

Brady put on a proud smile. "It's hidden where no one would ever find it. My treasure box, buried under a rock, under our deck. Grown-ups can't even fit under the deck."

Wiki whistled low. "Impressive." Brady did a little curtsy.

"Any idea where Blackbeard is?" I asked Wiki.

Wiki sighed, took off his glasses, and rubbed the bridge of his nose. "Well, it doesn't matter where he is, because we all know where he's going to end up."

"Jail?" I asked.

"Your house," Wiki said.

Brady and I sat up, and I gulped loudly. "Um, what?"

"Think about it, guys. Blackbeard isn't a loner. He

operates with a crew. At the height of his infamy, his crew numbered in the hundreds, and he terrorized the seas with them."

"So he misses them and he wants to go home?" I asked.

"No, Javi. He's going to try to use Andy to summon them. And terrorize our world."

I felt like Brady had just punched me in the gut.

"So we need to figure out how we're gonna kick Blackbeard's bearded butt," Brady said, cracking her knuckles.

"That's where I'm stuck," Wiki said. "I think—"

"Hello, friends," a wicked, grizzled voice behind us said. A full shiver rode down my spine. We turned around slowly, because we recognized the voice.

Leaning on a tree was none other than our larger-than-life archnemesis, looking deadlier and creepier than ever. His beard could probably swallow us whole.

"Blackbeard!" I yelled, stating the obvious. "Where'd you come from?"

"Are you a ghost, a ninja, or a ninja-ghost?" Brady asked, wide-eyed.

Blackbeard chuckled darkly. "I followed you three here. I've been watching you."

"No more talking! Run!" I screamed. We took off.

"Wait!" the pirate boomed. And his voice was so commanding, it was like he cast a spell—we froze in place, not even three steps away from him.

His voice softened. "I'm not here to hurt you. I'm here to thank you."

"Uhh...what did he say?" I asked Wiki, as we turned around.

"You saved my life, after all," Blackbeard said as he took a few steps closer.

Wiki gasped. "Robert Maynard. That's why you threw the book to the ground. You read about—"

"My untimely and grisly death. Yes." Blackbeard nodded. "A more violent death than I ever inflicted on any of my victims," he muttered angrily.

"How does he die?" Brady whispered to Wiki.

"He gets his head cut off after getting shot five times and then stabbed twenty-six times. Oh, and then they mount his head on the front of a ship."

"Yiiiiiiikes," I whispered, rubbing my neck.

"I'm not going back to that dreadful fate," Blackbeard said gruffly.

Awesome. Fantastic. We were stuck with him.

"Now, you have something which I require," he said calmly as he rubbed his beard with one hand. "And because you've accidentally saved my life, I won't take it the way I usually take things. Instead, I will merely ask."

He took out a sword and we gasped—but then he pushed the tip into the ground and leaned on it like a cane.

"You have three days to bring me the bell."

"The bell?!" Brady shrieked. "No way, José! You're not—"

"Stop!" Blackbeard barked. Then he calmed back down. "Don't say anything you'll regret, future pirate queen. Three days is a generous amount of time. Think it over." He chuckled. "You'll find you have no choice."

"Why three days?" I said, thinking out loud. "Why not just make us get it now?"

"Javi, shh!" Wiki whispered. "He's a nefarious villain. He likes being dramatic. And he likely has a larger plan."

Brady pushed her lips together and growled at Beardo.

"Now SHOO!" he snarled, slicing the air with his sword.

We practically flew.

12

The rest of that day was a blur. I'm sure teachers said stuff, and if they asked me questions I probably answered them, but I don't remember it at all. Wiki, Brady, and I didn't even say a word to each other as we walked home. Dinner was super quiet too, as much as Dad tried to get us to talk about our day. And when we finally went to bed, I just stared at the ceiling.

There were three thoughts going through my head (in fast-forward, on repeat) all day:

1. Welp, being alive was pretty awesome, and I had a good run for a solid twelve years, but adios, life! The most ferocious pirate of all time is hunting us down and is three days from killing us. Scarf

down all the sandwiches you can, because you are done-zo!

2. Wait wait wait. Staying alive is easy, Javi. Just give that nice pirate the bell and you can live a full life, fulfill your goal of eating a nine-foot sub solo, and retire as a world-famous chef one day. Sure, Blackbeard and his crew might take over the world and we'd all have to sing sea chanteys instead of saying the Pledge of Allegiance, but is that so bad? Sea chanteys are kind of catchy!

3. Or...you could actually be brave for once and do what you know you've got to do: stop Blackbeard. Would this probably lead to an even worse death at the hands of a homicidal pirate? Most definitely! In fact, you'd probably have a 0.00000001 percent chance of coming out on top. But if you did it, you'd be a hero, and they'd shower you with tostones!

Most of the day, I was going with Option 2, then

during dinner I was toying with Option 3, but quickly went back to Option 2.

The next morning I woke up with the best option of all: Option 4.

4. This whole thing was just a dream! Stop eating cheesesteaks at night, Javi—they give you the weirdest nightmares!

Ah, good old trusty Option 4. It made the morning a breeze. I whistled as I brushed my teeth, ate my breakfast sandwich while humming a tune, stepped outside to get the newspaper for Dad with a big smile on my face, nodded as I ignored the huge pirate flag draped across our lawn, whistled again as I put my books in my backpack, got ready for school.

WAIT.

A HUGE PIRATE FLAG DRAPED ACROSS OUR LAWN?

I ran to the front door and opened it again. There was a big, black-and-white, skull-and-crossbones-style flag lying a few feet in front of our welcome mat.

Okay, there went Option 4. It was nice while it lasted.

"So who's excited to give Blackbeard his bell?" I asked, laughing nervously. "I know I am. Anyone else? Show of hands?"

Brady gave me a death glare and Wiki just shook his head. We were eating lunch in the corner of the cafeteria. I'd just told Wiki about the flag, then he told us that he didn't have a plan for beating the pirate yet. So surrendering had to be the only option.

"Javi, we have three days," Brady whispered loudly. "Wiki can concentrate on making a plan, I can train for the ultimate showdown, and you can...feed us."

"Actually, I'll need your help researching," Wiki said. He looked like he hadn't slept yet again. "I'll be the first to admit that pirates are one of my most sizable knowledge gaps. I find them to be puerile."

"Huh?"

"Childish and silly. Not worth serious research. But now that our lives depend on it..." Wiki sighed. "Well, we need to find something we can use against him."

"Can't we just call the cops? Or tell our teachers?" I asked. "Is that too easy an option for you?"

"I've given that option a lot of thought, and it's the most dangerous of all," Wiki said. "Any adults who stop Blackbeard will find out about Andy, force us to give them the bell, and before you know it, we'll have pirates and knights and who knows what else destroying the world."

"Yeah." I nodded. "Good point. Just like in the movies. Adults ruin everything."

"News flash!" Brady said, waving her hands in Wiki's face. "You know what would stop Blackbeard better than a bunch of cops and teachers? Heroes that we summon through Andy."

Wiki shook his head quickly. "I thought we'd closed this line of discussion. We are NOT using Andy again. Do you know what would happen if we did? We'd probably end up summoning a monster."

"Did somebody say *monster*?!"

Brady gasped, I jumped, and Wiki screamed. Standing in front of us, smiling his wickedest smile, was none other than Blackbeard! He was as terrifying as ever. And he was holding...a mop?

"Surprised to see me?" Blackbeard asked. "Thought

I'd patiently wait in the woods until you rustled up that bell?"

He leaned down, got right up in my face, and whispered in his slowest, nastiest whisper, "Now, save me a few days and kindly give me what I seek." He looked at each of us in turn. I was pretty sure I was going to wet my pants, and Wiki looked like he already had. Brady just crossed her arms and gave him a stubborn look. Blackbeard then shot one hand up like he was about to grab my collar, when he was interrupted by a loud pat on his back.

"Ah, Mr. Teach, I see you're introducing yourselves to the students," Principal Gale said kindly but firmly.

Principal Gale is our fearless leader—the head of the whole school. She's been at Finistere forever (seriously, no one remembers the school without her), but she still doesn't look any older than Dad. She's one of those super-principals who knows every student's name and birthday and hangs out in the library after school to help kids out with their homework. Parents love her, teachers think she's rad, and kids wish she was less awesome so we could make fun of her. (It's deeply unsettling to actually love your principal.) She's sunny and smiley and always fair, but you get the feeling that you don't ever want to get on her bad side. Plus, there are rumors that she keeps mythical beasts in the dungeon. And no one wants to meet a bloodthirsty dragon face-to-face down there.

"Yes, just doing my best to meet all of these wonderful students," Blackbeard said with an awkward, forced smile. "Such sweet lads. Delighted to meet you three. Er...study hard, chaps!"

"Kids, meet our new groundskeeper, Mr. Teach. He'll be helping to make our school a cleaner, better environment for learning." We nodded nervously, trying to be polite, screaming on the inside. "We're honored to have such a passionate new member of our community. He's already planning on building new facilities for students. Wait until you hear about his plans for a puppy-petting room!" *Blackbeard* and *puppies* in the same sentence? "Now come with me for a bit, Edward—something's wrong with the toilets in the teachers' bathroom." Blackbeard frowned to himself, then smiled weakly at the principal and nodded. As they walked off,

Blackbeard turned to us and held up one finger. "*Day one*," he mouthed. Then he gave us a menacing smile. The fact that some of his teeth were black or missing made it way more menacing.

13

We spent the rest of the school day on high alert. Twice during math class, Wiki and I noticed Blackbeard peeking through the hall window into our classroom as he mopped. Then, during science, he was sweeping the playground outside our classroom, and every time I looked out he met my eyes with a dark smile.

We were in gym class playing kickball and Wiki pointed subtly to the bleachers at the other side of the gym. There was Blackbeard sitting with a shovel across his lap and staring at us like we had targets on our foreheads.

"I can't take much more of this, Wiki," I whispered while we waited in line to kick the ball.

He nodded. "Is he going to give us three days? He's clearly not a patient man. And pirates weren't known for their honesty."

"Also, how are we going to make a plan if he's always around the corner watching us?"

"He might follow us home," Wiki whispered. "Clearly he remembers where we live."

"Oh right!" I whispered back. "Ugh, I don't want to see him standing in the middle of my backyard at night. That's nightmare fuel for life."

I looked over at Piratey McPirateFace and he was still staring straight at us. "By the way, I hope pirates can't read lips."

"We're as good as dead," Wiki said.

"We're as good as dead," I repeated.

"JAVIER SANTIAGO. BRADY SANTIAGO. WILL GREEN. PLEASE REPORT TO THE OFFICE!" the intercom blared.

"Oooooooh," chanted the class. "Someone's in trouble..."

More like someone just got their life saved! I've never been happier about having to report to the principal.

Wiki and I practically skipped all the way to the high school. And you know who didn't follow us? His name rhymes with "Frackbleard."

"Have a seat, children," Principal Gale said as we walked into her office.

When I say "principal's office" you're probably thinking gross vomit-green carpet, dumb posters of cats saying stuff like "Hang In There!" and boring office supplies all lined up neatly on an old desk. This was the opposite of that. Principal Gale's office looked like it belonged to Merlin. It was in the castle, so the walls, floor, and ceiling were all made of stone. Two enormous torches lit the room, giving it the vibe of a haunted house when the curtains were drawn. There were all sorts of ornate tools and instruments hanging from the walls, some of which I'd never seen before in a museum or a book. In one corner there was a big cage covered by some fancy fabric. (Everyone had theories about what lived in the cage.) Principal Gale's stone desk looked like it was right at home in a castle, and her chair was actually a throne that felt like it belonged to King Arthur. On her desk she had an emerald orb that matched the emerald necklace she always wore. All in all, it was almost impossible to pay attention to Principal Gale while you were in there, because your eyes kept wandering to all the awesome stuff everywhere.

"Thanks so much for heading over so quickly, and apologies for interrupting your classes," the principal said sweetly. "How is your week going so far?"

"Um...great! Yeah, good, really good. Having a great week, thanks. Really, really top-notch. Weeks are awesome. I love weeks. Weeks." The stupid words just kept plopping out of my mouth. Everyone gave me a weird look.

"It's been pretty good," Brady said, trying to save me from my own awkwardness.

"I would give it a solid eight, if one is dreadful and ten is superlative," Wiki echoed, nodding.

Principal Gale kept her smile, but I could see the tiniest hint of suspicion forming at the edges of it.

"Excellent. Glad to hear it," she continued. "I was curious about your thoughts on our new groundskeeper, Mr. Teach."

Gulp.

"M-m-mister Teach? W-who is that?" Wiki squeaked, trying to play dumb but just looking dumb instead.

"He seems all right," Brady said calmly. Why was Brady the master of staying cool under pressure? Did she go to spy school on the weekends?

"I see," the principal said slowly.

Awkward silence.

"I must say, when I stumbled onto your conversation with him, it appeared to me that you'd met before. Have you? Perhaps he's a neighbor or a family friend?"

"Blackbeard, a family friend? Hah! That's hilarious!" I said, before realizing what had just come out of my mouth.

Brady and Wiki shot daggers at me with their eyes. I'd seen Brady's look before. The way she squinted meant, "Are you really that stupid?"

"We've never met him before. Seems like a nice enough guy," Brady said blandly.

Another awkward silence. I couldn't look Principal Gale in the eye, so I just stared at her necklace.

"Has anything strange happened to you three over the past week? Anything at all?"

I stopped myself from saying something dumb this time, but my eyes went super wide, which was maybe even dumber than all the other things I said before.

"Strange?" Brady looked over at me. "My brother's a weirdo, so life is always strange with him around. But other than his extreme weirdness, nothing else strange."

"Yes, I concur. Nothing odd about this week at all," Wiki said, maybe a little too quickly.

The awkwardest silence of all. This one seemed to last forever.

"Well, all right then. I brought you up here because I thought you'd met Mr. Teach before, and I wanted you to know that our new groundskeeper is a bit rough around the edges. He had a difficult past. But he's a changed man. He apologized for his past behavior and wants nothing more than to live a peaceful life with our community."

Was that the lie Blackbeard fed her? I wanted to say something, but I'd already opened my mouth too many times, so I just stared blankly at Principal Gale. So did Brady and Wiki. More awkward silence.

"In any event, thanks so much for coming to see

me. If you change your minds, or if something strange happens and you have no one you feel comfortable telling, please don't hesitate to see me. My door is always open."

"Th-th-thank you!" Wiki said as we all quickly got up and started making our way out the door.

"One more thing," Gale said right before we were out the door.

We turned around nervously.

"Javi, that was a great essay you wrote for Ms. Vlad. It was so creative, but it felt so real. You deserved that A++."

She read my essay? I nodded awkwardly, made a funny noise, and we stumbled out of the room.

I felt so confused, embarrassed, and dumb that I was dizzy and couldn't say anything. Wiki was probably just feeling confused. But Brady snapped us out of it.

"Guys, it's five minutes before the bell rings and school's over. If we just head straight into the woods from here, we might lose Blackbeard."

"Brilliant idea, Brady," Wiki said as we tiptoed down the high school stairwell. "However, we need to devour every book written about Blackbeard and pirates. And we're right next to the best place in town to do that."

"Then let's make a run for it," I said. "Now!" We dashed down one hall, took a left, and then caught our breath as we walked calmly into the high school library.

14

Finistere's library is massive and windowless, with walls made of stone and ceilings so high you can't see them. It's a cross between an endless cave and a sorcerer's basement. The bookshelves aren't exactly kid-friendly either—there must be fifteen rows of books on them, and I can only reach the first three, maybe four, on my tippy-toes. Otherwise you have to ask Mr. Bottom the librarian to bring over his ginormous iron ladder, which makes an ear-piercing squeak whenever he wheels it around. And yeah, his name is Mr. Bottom. We called him Mr. Butt behind his back for a few weeks when we first met him, but he's way too nice, so we stopped.

"Might I be of assistance, Master Green?" Mr. Bottom

asked as we walked past the front desk toward the stacks. Mr. B had a thick British accent and talked and dressed like an English prince from the olden days. He knew Wiki super well because Wiki basically lived at the library after school.

"Hi, Mr. Bottom. I need to do some research on pirates. I'm guessing the Dewey Decimal Number is in the low nine hundreds?"

"Nine hundred and ten, to be precise. Well done! I imagine that you'll be wanting primary sources only, per usual?"

Wiki nodded. "Translation, Wiki?" Brady whispered.

"I want the original books written about pirates, not the kiddie stuff that summarizes it."

Brady rolled her eyes. Mr. B took us through a few tall shelves toward the back wall of the library. The back of the library was kind of spooky, because there were fewer torches, and it got pretty dark and dank. You could barely read the names of books back there. If Mr. B was with you, it didn't really matter though, because he'd basically memorized every single book in the library. And there must have been a million books.

The iron ladder was only a few shelves away, so Mr. B wheeled it over and then climbed to the very top. Wiki explained that most of the old books in the library were hidden away at the top shelf where only Mr. B could access them. It can't be normal for a school library to have ancient books, but at Finistere it didn't even surprise me.

"Hmmm...book...book...my kingdom for that book... Aha! Here is the very tome I'm looking for." Mr. B pulled out a tome, and even in the darkness I could see the dust flutter around it. He climbed down the stairs and presented it to Wiki like it was treasure. "Master Green, may I present you with the classic text, *A General History of the Robberies and Murders of the Most Notorious Pyrates.*"

"Hmm," Wiki said. "I'm embarrassed to admit that I haven't read this one." Brady rolled her eyes again.

"An interesting tidbit, then. Most of our knowledge of pirates comes from this single source. One book to explain such a rich and riotous period of our history—it boggles the mind, no?"

Wiki nodded as he flipped to the first page. I looked over his shoulder and it read:

As the Pyrates in the Weſt Indies have been ſo formidable that they have interrupted the Trade of Europe into thoſe parts...

Was this even in English?!

"Mr. B," I said, raising my hand for some reason. "Can Brady and I read the kids' pirate books?"

An hour later we were the only ones in the library, huddled over a few books that we'd laid out on one of the desks next to the shelves. Wiki read lightning fast, so he'd made it through most of his old book and part of another one while Brady and I were just finishing the Blackbeard chapter of our pirate books.

"If we're looking for his kryptonite, I'm not really seeing much," I said. "Honestly, I'm just a thousand percent more scared now that I know what this guy was like back then. He used to light his beard on fire before attacking a ship! And in Mexico they called him El Gran Diablo—The Great Devil."

"Unfortunately, this text isn't helping much either," Wiki said, finally looking up from his book. "Not a lot is known about Blackbeard himself, only his dastardly acts. Here's what I jotted down. What have you got?"

After comparing notes, this is what we knew:

1. Blackbeard was no dummy. Historians were pretty sure he was well-educated and a big reader. There were tons of books found on his ship.

2. The dude had no fear. Beardo got his reputation in less than a year of piracy because he took over harbors, set ports on fire, and hijacked ships that were way bigger than his.

3. And what a reputation! Freakbeard was America's nightmare. He scared colonial Americans more than anyone else in existence. Even more than a comet, one writer from back then said. (I guess comets were super scary in pirate times.)

4. He preferred intimidation to violence. Apparently the scariest guy in the world didn't love killing people as much as scaring the pants off them.

"Wait, wait, wait," Brady said after Wiki revealed that last point. "So he's all bark and no bite? What are we afraid of then? I'm all bite and no bark!" Brady started looking for something to roundhouse kick.

"Don't get cocky," Wiki said. "He's got plenty of bite. Pirates were constantly taking over ships, but attacking a ship meant you'd ruin it before you stole it. Intimidate your enemy and the ship stays good as new. Intimidation was a smarter tactic." Wiki let out a long sigh. "Honestly, I'd rather he was more bloodthirsty and violent. He is far more cunning an opponent than I imagined. The way he charms his enemies and then backstabs them is particularly alarming."

"Well, you heard the principal," I said. "He's pretending to be Mr. Smiley Nice Guy Pirate to the teachers while he's Mr. Stabby Murderfest Pirate to us. And so far the teachers seem to be buying it."

"Shh!" Brady said. She walked forward a few steps and peered down a long line of shelves. Then she motioned to us.

Standing in front of a desk, reading a huge map laid out on it by torchlight, was Mr. Teach himself. Mr. B was standing next to him and answering his questions. Blackbeard kept pointing to different areas as Mr. B spoke and nodded. He had his hand on Mr. B's shoulder, in full Friendly Pirate mode.

"What's he up to?" Brady whispered.

"I'm not sure," Wiki whispered back. "But he's definitely learning all he can about the modern world."

"And how to take it over," I added.

At that, Blackbeard looked up and we scrambled all the way home in a full sprint.

15

Someone knocked on our door around 8:00 p.m., and when I looked through the peephole, I was almost positive I'd see Beardo with his sword pointed straight at me. Dad and Brady were in their rooms, so I was bracing myself for death. Instead it was Aunt Nancy, and for a second the world was lollipops and rainbows.

"Why, good evening, Javier. Is Wiki with you?" she asked sweetly (though she always wore an impish smile).

"Hey, Aunt Nancy. We were at the library until late. I think he said he was going straight home after that?"

She nodded. "Oh, that's right, that's right. I think

his mom mentioned that. Thanks, Javi." She waved and turned to go, but as I was closing the door she pointed a finger to the air.

"Ooh, I just remembered—I've been meaning to get that mofongo recipe from you. I'm thinking of making it for a little get-together tomorrow. Would you mind writing it out for me?"

Think about cooking instead of bloodthirsty pirates gutting me? Yes, please. I opened the door wide and motioned for her to come in. "My absolute pleasure, Aunt Nancy."

We walked to the kitchen, and I dug through the kitchen drawers for a pen and pad while she took a nice, long look around the living room and kitchen.

"There's something different about this house," she said, her eyes going from the couches to the bookshelves to the kitchen table. "Aha!" She patted Andy, and Andy purred.

I dropped my pen and looked over at her nervously, but she didn't seem to hear it.

"This is a magnificent piece of furniture," she said as she inspected the patterns carved into Andy's sides.

She shook the table. "Solid too. Where did you acquire this beauty?"

I plopped on the chair next to her to write the recipe. "Oh man, Dad takes us to so many antique stores and flea markets, I lose track. This one was far away, kind of in the middle of nowhere."

Aunt Nancy was lost in thought for a minute. I scribbled down the ingredients. "How many people are you cooking for?" I asked.

"Hmm? Oh, just four of us." She tapped on the recipe as I scribbled. "Remember the version of mofongo we had a month ago? You experimented with some spices on it. That's the one I want to make."

"Oh yeah! That might have been my all-time best. What spice was that?" I got up to check the spice rack as Aunt Nancy kept studying the table.

"Javi, I think you finally have a table worthy of your skills," she said. "That's an important step in any chef's journey."

She walked over to the spice rack but stopped in front of the fridge where Dad had posted my A++ essay. She picked it up and skimmed it as I went from spice to spice. Not coriander...not nutmeg... I used garlic in everything...

"It makes me happy to see you write about something so passionately," she said.

"Ginger! It was just ginger. But next time I'm planning to mix the plantains with yuca. I've heard that's a killer combo. You could try that too." She smiled and nodded and then I realized she had complimented me. "Oh, thanks." I blushed. "Probably the first time Javi the Stomach gets a decent grade in all of sixth grade."

She furrowed her brow, walked up to me, and looked me straight in the eye. "Hmmm. You don't yet see it, do you?" She lifted my chin up to really study my eyes. It felt like she was rummaging around in my soul.

"See what?" I yelped.

"You will soon," she said, turning to the table, grabbing the recipe, and making her way to the door. "You will soon."

As she opened the door to let herself out, she held up the recipe. "Ginger it is! Bring over some of the yuca mofongo when you make it. Or invite me over to dine on your distinguished new table. I'm glad you found one worthy of your talents."

She closed the door behind her, and for some reason everything in my life felt good for a solid three minutes.

16

I had some pretty weird dreams that night. I was the captain of a giant rubber duckie I'd named *Quacky's Revenge*, and I was sailing it through the Sea of Tubbé (which I'm pretty sure was just a giant bathtub). Then Blackbeard showed up in an enormous pirate ship built of beard hair and poked my duckie with his sword, deflating it. "Quacky, noooooo!" I yelled as we sank to the bottom of the sea and got sucked down a giant drain.

"Quacky!" I screamed as I shot up in bed the next morning.

"Quacky?" Brady asked, poking her head in my door. "You get weirder every day." Then she went downstairs.

"Great start to the day, Javi," I mumbled to myself as I got out of bed. "Fantastic start. A+."

Then I noticed the voices downstairs. Women's voices. For a second I thought Mom had come home early, but none of the voices were even semi-recognizable. I walked to the dining room slowly, not sure what to expect, and when I made it there I saw one of the most bizarre scenes I'd ever witnessed.

Sitting around the table were Brady and two other women, chitchatting as they ate scones and drank tea. They were clearly summoned by Andy, because neither looked like they belonged in our century. One of them I was unsure about, but the second one was obviously—

"Cleopatra," Brady said, "Rosa Parks, this is my brother Javi. Javi, these are the two awesomest women in history."

They must have nodded hello, but I was too busy yelling, "Brady! Are you bananas?! We're not supposed to—"

"Use Andy? Relax, bro. I'm not inviting pirates and murderers. You got to invite your three favorites to dinner, I just thought I'd invite my three to breakfast."

Three? I only saw two. Then I noticed that Brady was petting something under the table. A dog. Why did that dog look so familiar?

"Brady, is that..."

"Fluffers? Yep. Isn't he even fluffier than he seems on TV?"

"That's Fluffers?" I asked, my eyes saucers. "As in the president's dog, Fluffers. You stole the president of the United States' dog?!"

She glared at me. "I invited him, Javi. He's a guest. The fluffiest guest ever, aren't you, Fluffers? Aren't you?" she cooed, tickling his chin. Then she glared at me again. "It's just for an hour. Also, you don't think Cleopatra and Rosa Parks are more impressive than a pet? Do you know what our lives would be like if Rosa Parks hadn't existed?"

"You let your brother talk to you like this?" Cleopatra asked, scowling at me.

"Not usually," she said. "Don't worry, he's afraid of me."

"Good," she said, smiling regally. "Remember what I told you, Brady. You are a queen. I know a queen when I see one. And you are a queen."

"That's for sure," Rosa Parks said. "Want some scones, Javi? There's plenty to go around."

I scratched my neck awkwardly. "Um, thanks, but I'm good... Nice to meet you both, by the way. Hey Brady, we're going to be late for school."

"Education is the most important thing," Rosa Parks said.

"Especially for a future queen," Cleopatra added.

"Ugh, fine, Javi. Well, I'll invite you ladies for a follow-up lunch soon," Brady said brightly. "Thanks for hanging out."

I walked back upstairs as they all said their goodbyes, and then I heard the bell ring. Wow, would Wiki be furious if he found out. No way I was telling him.

I went to my room to get dressed, and when I shut the door I saw it for the first time. A big, dirty knife was stabbed into the inside of my bedroom door. It was holding up a note that said:

Your uniform today. OR ELSE.

Behind it were the rubber duckie pj's Abuela gifted me for my bday.

"Brady!" I yelled. "This is a truly sick prank!"

She walked into my room. "Prank? I wish I'd played a prank on you—I can't believe how rude you were to my guests." She glanced over at the knife, then walked up and took a long look at it. "No, that's definitely Blackbeard's knife. I recognize it from dinner. He's got pretty fancy handwriting for a pirate, don't you think?"

I screamed so loud I should have fainted.

"Javi, relax!" Brady yelled. "Deep breaths, okay? We're going to be late for school. Wiki's going to be here any minute, and we have a lot to talk about."

"Like the fact that Blackbeard broke into my room last night?" I asked, between screams. "Guess who's never sleeping in their bed again? This guy." I poked my finger into my chest.

"If he'd tried to sneak into my room"—Brady muttered, balling her hands into fists—"this whole thing would've been over. Bam!" She did a few karate punches while I pulled the knife out of the door.

I picked up the pj's from the floor. They were even

more humiliating than I remembered. Today was going to be the worst.

———

"So there are no signs of a break-in?" Wiki asked as we walked to school that morning, worried but also trying his best not to laugh at me.

"None," said Brady, also snickering. "He didn't touch Andy, and the bell is safe. Honestly, if he hadn't planted his knife in the door, we wouldn't even know someone had been in there."

"He truly is the king of psychological warfare," Wiki said, clearly impressed. "I can't imagine a worse thing to do to a middle schooler."

"Thanks, Wiki," I grumbled.

"You could've worn your normal clothes," Brady said. "He would have just challenged you to a friendly duel at recess. To the death, of course." She and Wiki broke into hysterical laughter. I'd like to say that it was nice to hear them laughing after so many serious days, but it wasn't. At all. I just gritted my teeth and soldiered on.

School started exactly like I expected it to. First

period Spanish was the worst. Buddy Grimes called me El Ducko the whole time, the class couldn't stop laughing, and Señor Q didn't even do anything to shut him up. To add to the nightmare, my secret crush, Sarah, was in that class. She didn't full-on laugh at me, but she did grimace a few times. Once we started our assignment, Señor Q asked me to come to his desk.

"Ese no es un nene, ese es un monstruo, Javier," he said. ("That's not a kid, that's a monster.") He liked that we could talk Spanish to each other, and usually that would mean we'd have a classic teacher-student friendship, but Q was strange even by Finistere's standards. Saying that he had an active imagination would be putting it mildly. "You need to put on your armor, grab your sword, and defeat the monster," he said very seriously in Spanish.

You would think that'd be a good pep talk, but Q wasn't trying to tell me to be brave. He literally thought I owned armor and a sword and I should wear them. And he probably believed that Grimes was a bona fide monster. "Um, okay, Señor Q. I'll bring my...armor... next time."

"Buenisimo," he said, clapping me on the back. "Mi heroe." Yeah right, like I was anyone's hero.

Ms. Vlad was next, and it wasn't an improvement. She raised an eyebrow when I walked into class two seconds after the bell, and everyone noticed my getup and laughed. Then, while she went to the printer room to get our homework, Grimes stood on his chair and said, "I vant to suck your ducks!" in his best Dracula impression. The class went into hysterics, and even though I should've been embarrassed, I was actually terrified. Everyone always made fun of my Vlad vampire theory, but not in the middle of class. I was 95 percent sure Vlad was going to chomp Grimes's neck in a vampiric rage and turn him full bloodsucker in front of all of us. But the class had settled down by the time she returned.

Art was third and it was a little bit better. Ms. Calderon has zero patience for bullying or meanness of any kind. When I walked into class she looked me up and down and gave me a thumbs-up. "I am impressed, Javier," she said, nodding. "Finally you are starting to let your fashion sense show." She pointed over to our easels. "And your timing is perfect—we begin our self-portraits today."

Ms. Calderon was my favorite teacher. Wiki liked her too, but for completely different reasons. I loved that she was a real artist. When we painted, she painted. And she was so into it—she thought about painting the same way I thought about cooking. It was something you worked hard at, but it didn't feel like work, and it was worth it anyway because the final product was so awesome. She was also super creative and really encouraged us to find our own styles. No art was bad art if it was true to your style. That's how I felt about cooking, mostly.

Wiki dug her because she was secretly tough as nails. You barely saw it, because usually Ms. Calderon was super sweet, but no one even dreamed of messing with her. I was pretty sure that she was a warrior by night and she would one day train Brady in the ways of butt-kicking.

A few of the girls in class started quacking at me as we started painting, but Ms. C gave them one of her signature looks and they shut up immediately. Part of Ms. C's toughness comes from her eyes. She has such an intense stare when she's painting or talking about painting that

I think it's going to light the canvas on fire. The other kids make fun of it behind her back, but I think it's kind of awesome and the root of her powers. I remember when we were finishing each other's portraits one day and she talked about how your eyes should pierce the painting. The other kids laughed but I dug it.

"A self-portrait isn't just about painting yourself," she said as she walked around the room. "It is about painting your presence. Your essence. What makes you unique. Whether you illustrate it in the expression, the lighting, the objects, or landscape surrounding you." She nodded as she passed by each kid's painting.

"We need to expand our search," Wiki whispered to me. We were painting next to each other. "I'm not sure my pirate research surfaced anything useful. We need a new approach." I glanced at his self-portrait, which looked like a stick figure. Wiki was a genius, but a lousy artist.

"Okay, let's see..." I whispered when Ms. Calderon was on the other side of the room. "Maybe we study things that sailors are scared of? Ooh, we could use Andy to summon a giant squid."

Wiki made a face. "I'm picturing a giant squid slithering around helplessly in your kitchen. Ew, that's disgusting." He shook his head. "No, I was thinking about the other defining aspect of Blackbeard. He's a pirate, but he's also technically a chrononaut."

"A cronut? Wow, just realized I'm starving." I licked my lips.

"A chrononaut. A time traveler. I mean, I don't know exactly how Andy functions, but regardless, there are a lot of things Blackbeard won't understand about the modern world. And I bet technology will scare him. We can use that to our advantage."

Thirty minutes later, Wiki had proven his point. We were at library class in the dumpy middle school library. (Picture a boring school library. Yep, that's it. It's nothing like the magical high school library.) We were trying to research time travel, but this library only had books that were middle school level or below, so we weren't finding much.

Blackbeard was sitting at the computers twenty feet away from us, and the middle school librarian was helping him figure out what he was doing.

"Wow, I can't believe you want to spend your weekends building a puppy-petting area for the kids." She swooned. "You really are as bighearted as they say." The librarian's eyes looked like they could have had little cartoon hearts in them. I groaned quietly.

"Yes, anything for the, er...kids. They are our, uh, future," Blackbeard mumbled, clearly trying not to throw up in his mouth as he said it. "Now, is this the compass then?" he asked, waving the mouse in the air and shaking it. "It doesn't seem to be working. I don't see true north. Your compass is broken."

The librarian shook her head. "That's not a compass, it's a—"

"A very small telescope. Yes, I see that now. Hmmm, I don't see the hole..." He put the mouse up to his eye. "Oh no. I'm mistaken. This is clearly a tiny anchor." He tossed it onto the floor, then shook his head and looked at her. "This is a very low-quality anchor. I suggest you invest in better anchors."

I was trying my hardest not to laugh.

"Why are all the teachers here so bad at technology?" the librarian muttered under her breath as she put the mouse back on the table and explained computers to Mr. Teach. He started trying to order the monitor around like it was one of his crew.

"I have to sit somewhere else," I wheezed. "Or I'm going to explode."

Wiki held it together better than I did. "As funny as this is, we're still watching him gather information for world domination." He looked over at me. "But this does confirm my suspicion. We can use a version of the Columbus eclipse approach."

"You know I have no idea what that is," I said, looking down at the table so I wouldn't laugh at Beardo.

"Christopher Columbus once used his knowledge of an upcoming eclipse to fool the Indigenous people into thinking God stole the sun because He was mad at them. Columbus predicted the sun's vanishing to their chief and it terrified them. Really he'd just read about it in an almanac."

"Wow, that guy really was the worst. But your point is?"

"There are a thousand ways we can use technology to scare someone from the seventeen hundreds. We're talking about pre–Industrial Revolution times. Even a telephone or car is news to them." I nodded. Wiki did have a point. "Okay, give me some time to come up with a plan," he said. He did some mental calculations in his head, then noticed something behind me. "Hey Javi, check it out. Looks like we're not the only Blackbeard haters."

I turned around, and sitting in a corner of the library with a newspaper in his lap was none other than Mr. Scrimshaw. And he had a death stare aimed right at everyone's favorite pirate. "Finally, someone who sees through him!" I wanted to walk over and high-five him right then and there, but he already thought I was weird enough. Still, it was good to know that one teacher in this school had common sense.

The day was finally looking up, when a bunch of girls leaving the library whispered, "Quack you later, loser."

Gym was last period. Right before the bell rang I was putting away the kickball in the storage room when I heard someone behind me. The way the hairs stood up on my neck, I knew exactly who it was.

"Day two," Blackbeard said darkly as he pretended to mop the floor.

Instead of my usual terrified self, I was actually mad. "This is a low blow, even for you! Why didn't you make Brady wear some dumb pj's too?"

"And upset the future Queen of Pirates? Never." Blackbeard smiled. "But please never wear that to school again. It's even worse than I imagined."

"I wasn't planning on it."

Then in one second his face went from weird smile to violent frown. "Enough. I grow impatient. Do you have the bell or not?"

In one second I went from angry Javi to petrified bunny rabbit. "W-w-we have one more d-d-day!"

"Today is the last day I ask nicely. And if I don't get it by the end of the school day tomorrow..." He walked off without finishing his thought. Not like he had to anyway.

"Wikiiiiiiii!" I yelled, running to catch him in the halls.

He better have come up with a solid plan. Or we were going to have to rethink this whole not-giving-Blackbeard-the-bell thing.

17

"**What would scare me if I were from the** seventeen hundreds?" Wiki asked himself, looking around Brady's room as she practiced flying side kicks and I lay on the floor, imagining our deaths. "Music playing from speakers, maybe? Or a voice seeming to emanate from nowhere?"

"It should probably be portable, Wiki," Brady said mid-kick. "Maybe you should steal your dad's phone."

"Smartphone. Yes, you're right. I won't need to steal it—he would love a day without it. Hmm, the possibilities are endless. I'll have to experiment with it tonight."

"Hey guys," I said, staring up at the ceiling. "Have you ever stopped to wonder exactly how Andy works?"

"Stopped to wonder?" Wiki asked, looking at me like I should be wearing a dunce cap. He pulled a notebook out of his backpack and started tearing out pages and tossing them at me. They landed like dirty snowflakes on my head, and I sat up to make sense of them. Wiki's class notes usually look like a mad scientist's scribbles, but these were extra loco. He had all kinds of diagrams scrawled across every page, mostly arrows pointing back and forth along a time line with a sketch of Andy somewhere in the middle.

"This is intense, even for you," Brady muttered as she picked up some of the pages and also tried making sense of them. "Why'd you get so obsessed with it?"

"Why?" Wiki gasped. "I'll tell you why. Because Mozart became the most famous musician of all time, the Earl of Sandwich invented the sandwich, and Blackbeard's still dead." We both stared at him blankly. "Haven't I explained the competing theories of time travel to you both ad nauseum?"

"Wiki, you know we tune you out the second you start ranting about time travel," Brady said flatly. "Just like when you bring up those Hadron Collider thingies."

"Fine, well then here's something to blow your mind:

What if Mozart became legendary because he saw what pianos were like in the future? What if the earl created the sandwich because Javi showed him one first?"

Our jaws dropped so hard I swear I heard them hit the floor.

"It's the butterfly effect. The tiniest change to the past can cause massive changes to the future. So when they went back to their original times, having learned about futuristic pianos and sandwiches, they could have totally changed our future. But that's just one theory. Because then there's the multiverse theory."

"You're making me dizzy again," Brady said, but Wiki ignored her.

"The multiverse theory states that our guests are either plucked from a parallel universe or returned to one, so that the other universe is changed, but ours remains untouched. This is a popular theory, and I'm almost positive it's how Andy works. Otherwise the butterfly effect would have done much worse things to our reality. Of course there are at least five other competing theories that seem viable to me."

"Wiki," Brady said, punctuating his name with a

stomp that made me worry we were going to fall through the floor. "Basta. Enough. Stop wasting your brain on time-travel theories and start using it to get us out of this mess. Focus on the bell."

That shut him up. We shared a long moment of silence watching Wiki nod in slow motion as his brain started working on the right problem again. It hypnotized me into a daydream about Andy.

"Speaking of the bell..." I said, as my brain landed on an idea. "Andy's a pretty old-looking table. Ancient, even. You ever think that we might not be the first people to use the bell?"

Wiki huffed. "Trust me, Javi, I've thought about that extensively too. The issue is, I imagine few people would escape like Blackbeard did, and if they did they must have been caught. Otherwise we would've heard of them. There are no news stories about historical figures reemerging into modern society."

Brady looked at me, nodding. "I don't know, Wiki. If someone was smart, they could probably figure out a way to disguise themselves and stick around. I think Javi might be onto something...for once."

"We can theorize about Andy after we've survived tomorrow," Wiki said flatly. "Let me focus on defeating the most fearsome pirate of all time."

"Th-th-that most fearsome pirate of all time?" I asked, as my heart practically exploded. Leaning against a tree in our front yard was an extremely smug Blackbeard, staring right at me through the window, eating an apple he'd stabbed with his knife. He pointed the knife at me, winked, and walked away.

18

"**Everyone in front of their easel, class**," Ms. Calderon said as we shuffled into the room.

It was first period, and Wiki still hadn't told us his plan. On the walk to school he'd said he thought it had a 64 percent chance of success, but he was still working out the kinks. I did the math—64 percent chance of success meant a 36 percent chance of us dying. That was a 36 percent bigger chance of death than I felt comfortable with. Brady wasn't too happy with that number either.

"You'll notice you have a brand-new canvas today, not yesterday's half-finished self-portrait," Ms. C said in her singsongy voice. "We will continue those tomorrow, but today we are going to be working on something else. We have a very special guest who volunteered to model for us—we'll be painting his portrait for our double-period art today."

Someone modeling for us? For almost two hours? This was going to be weird. Was it a high schooler? A teacher?

Then the smell wafted in.

No. Oh no. Please no.

"Perhaps you have not had the pleasure of meeting him yet, but already he is a legend at this school. Ever since he arrived, teachers are finding flowers on their desks in the morning and spotless classrooms that we can all appreciate. He has generously vowed to spend his weekends building new facilities for you to maximize your learning. And he just loves kids and puppies. May I present our wonderful new groundskeeper, Mr. Teach. Strike a pose on the little stage for us, Mr. Teach. Kids, give him a warm welcome."

Some kids applauded loudly, some gave some confused claps, and Wiki and I just stared in horror as Blackbeard clomped onto the little platform in front of us, sat on the stool, and smiled so widely at us that it seemed like his entire beard was grinning.

It was the creepiest smile I'd ever seen in my life. Oh, we were dead. So very dead.

"Feel free to find a pose that speaks to your essence, Mr. Teach," Ms. C said, moving her arms in the air to demonstrate. "And when you've found that pose, let us know and the kids will begin their artistic renderings."

"Ready," Blackbeard said, still smiling cruelly as he looked straight at Wiki and me and mouthed *"Day three."*

"Perhaps you could tell the kids a little bit about yourself, Mr. Teach, to help them conjure up your essence as they paint," Ms. C said nicely.

"I was born on the sea, I've spent my life on the sea, and one day I'll die on the sea. The sea is my mother, my father, my lover, and my child," Blackbeard said, way more poetically than I could've imagined.

Secret Crush Sarah raised her hand. "You look a lot like a pirate, Mr. Teach. But you don't talk like a pirate."

Blackbeard chuckled without smiling. "Now, how do you suppose a real pirate talks?"

"Oh, you know, 'Yarrrr matey! Shiver me timbers!

Avast! Walk the plank, landlubbers! You're headed to Davy Jones's Locker.' Like that," she said.

Blackbeard shook his head, puzzled. "I'm afraid I've never heard pirates talk like that."

Sarah looked shocked. "Really? At lunch I'll show you some videos of how pirates actually talk. Then maybe you can pretend you're a real pirate."

Blackbeard nodded slowly, perplexed.

Tommy raised his hand. "Are you obsessed with whales like Mr. Scrimshaw is?"

Blackbeard gave a wicked smile. "No, because I've never hunted whales. I hunt...other things."

His eyes landed on us again.

"Ms. C, bathroom!" I yelped, dashing out before she had time to say anything.

Wiki joined me in the hall a minute later. "Well, this is going to be an unpleasant morning."

"You think? That smile he just gave us. I think it was the Smile of Death."

"There's no such thing as a Smile of Death, Javi. Kiss of Death, yes. Smile of Death, no," Wiki said calmly.

"Can you please just tell me how we're defeating

Beardo after school? I could use a little ray of hope right about now."

"Well, hold on a second. This plan isn't meant to defeat Blackbeard just yet. It's just meant to buy me some time to concoct the bigger plan."

"This isn't the plan? It's the pre-plan to let you figure out THE PLAN?! Oh, we're dead. We are so very, completely, utterly, hopelessly dead." At this point I was walking in circles with my hands raised above my head, ranting at the ceiling. Finally I just marched back into art class and resumed my post five feet away from Blackbeard's death stare.

The rest of art class was probably the worst two hours of my life. Sarah spent half the class teaching Blackbeard to talk like the pirates on TV, and Blackbeard spent the rest of it talking about how there was nothing sweeter than revenge.

The school day flew past after that. I guess time flies when you're hours away from a gruesome death! At least Wiki was focused—every time I glanced at him during class he was hunched over his notebook scribbling diagrams and maps.

When the final bell rang, my heart stopped for a full minute.

Wiki, Brady, and I met at the middle school lockers. Wiki was staring at the floor, his eyes darting back and forth like he was reading invisible diagrams. Brady asked him over and over again to tell us the plan, but Wiki kept his intense floor-stare going, mumbling what sounded like math equations to himself. Brady turned to the drinking fountain next to us, filled her cupped hands with water, and splashed it in his face.

That did the trick. "Brady! Why?! Ugh, I hate getting wet! You know that's my pet peeve!"

"Who are you, the Wicked Witch of the West? Wake up. You better have the perfect plan cooked up or else we're all dead meat. Dead. Meat." Brady's finger was practically wedged in Wiki's cheek.

"Guys," I said. "It's too late."

Brady and Wiki followed my bulging eyes to the other end of the hallway, where who else was making his way toward us but one Edward "Blackbeard/Beardo/WeirdBeard" Teach. And he was wearing the most demented smile I'd ever seen. His eyes were squarely on our trio as he lurched toward us. Did I see a glimmer of steel under his belt? Was that a dagger?! I wanted to scream "Guess what, folks? Our new groundskeeper is a pirate whose hobbies include murder and dismemberment!" but I couldn't do anything but stare.

"If he doesn't kill us, I'm going to kill you," Brady said through clenched teeth to Wiki.

Then I noticed that Wiki was whispering something so quietly it was almost impossible to hear. "Come on... come on...come on..."

Blackbeard got closer. We stared dumbly at him, frozen. He was three classrooms away. Two classrooms. One. Here it comes—our untimely death...

"Mr. Teach." Principal Gale walked out of the classroom right in front of us. Blackbeard jumped. "I'm so glad I finally found you. It appears that Ms. Tsogyal sprained her ankle, and we need a substitute yoga instructor for the next few months. I've heard that you're very flexible."

"Flexible?" Blackbeard coughed, confused.

"Come with me, let me introduce you to the class. You can wear Ms. T's tights—she left them in the classroom. How familiar are you with downward dog?"

"What kind of a dog is that?"

The principal led him back down the hall, and then they disappeared around the corner.

The three of us looked at each other. Looked down the hall. Looked at each other. Looked down the hall. Looked at each other.

And *ran*.

19

My lungs were on fire, and my side was cramping, but that's what running for your life feels like, and I'm a pretty big fan of not being a corpse. The three of us were tearing through the woods at what felt like the speed of light, and I just kept my mind focused on the quadruple-decker sandwich I could make now that I wasn't living underground at the local cemetery. The yoga teacher prank was part one of Wiki's secret plan, and it was so brilliant and perfect and hilarious I didn't even ask about part two.

Wiki led us deeper and deeper into the woods and it kept getting darker and darker. Soon my sandwich dreams were interrupted by the memory of Blackbeard's

Smile of Death, which was 100 percent going to be etched into my soul for life. A shiver ran down my spine, which is a super weird feeling when you're running at full speed.

"There's no such thing as a Smile of Death. There's no such thing as a Smile of Death," I kept repeating to myself, closing my eyes and trying not to trip.

"Oh, there absolutely is," a gruff voice in front of us said. "Here it is again."

I opened my eyes to the ultimate terror. Blackbeard?! Impossibly, he emerged from behind a big tree trunk, his whole beard smiling cruelly as we skidded to a stop.

"But...but..." Wiki said, the sadness and fear in his face mixing weirdly.

"I postponed the class."

"Run!" Brady yelled, and we took off like a shot.

Blackbeard laughed. "Yarrrrrrrrr!" he yelled as he started chasing us through the dense woods. "Avast, mateys, you're headed for Davy Jones's locker! Ye'll be walking the plank in no time!"

"Why is Blackbeard suddenly talking like a TV

pirate?" Brady asked breathlessly while we sprinted, dodging trunks and roots.

Another moment where I would've laughed if we weren't about to be killed.

"Ye can't outrun me, ya scurvy landlubbers!" Blackbeard yelled. "My legs be twice as long as yours."

He was absolutely right. He was gaining on us quickly, and there was no way we'd make it another minute without his endless beard tackling us. Suddenly I cared a whole lot more about what Wiki had planned for part two.

"By the way, how's my pirate talk, ya hairy bilge rats? Convincing? Yarr-harr-harrrrrr!" he cackled. "I've been practicing all afternoon!"

"Very...convincing! A+ for effort!" Wiki yelled politely. Blackbeard smiled proudly. But he was probably still going to kill us.

"Okay, stop!" Wiki yelled, turning around quickly. The rest of us tried to stop on a dime and fell over, including Blackbeard. He shot right back up, though.

"Well, that was unnecessarily awkward. Now, hand me that bell," he said in a voice dripping with venom, as he drew his sword and pointed it down at me. My whole body went stiff. This was it. I was about to be sliced up into a human-sized enchilada.

"Watch out, Mr. Teach," Wiki said. "Or I'll summon your archnemesis. Do you seriously think the table's our only magic portal? Behold!" Wiki pulled out his dad's smartphone, pushed a button, and held it up to Blackbeard.

A video started playing. It was a close-up of a man's face. Wait, was that Wiki's dad? It took me a second to recognize the voice, but it was definitely Wiki's dad. "Blackbeard! Robert Maynard here. I'm looking forward to cutting your head off." Wiki must have told his dad this was for a school project. "But first, I want to introduce you to my associate. You might have heard of him. He's called...the Kraken!"

The Kraken, of course! The one sea monster that all pirates feared. The video cut to some terrifying movie footage of a giant squid attacking a pirate ship. If I were a pirate and I thought that was real, I would've ruined my pants.

Blackbeard looked confused, and maybe scared? It was hard to read his face through the endless beard

"Now leave us alone or I'll summon them both and you'll meet your grisly fate."

For a good five seconds I was sure Wiki had won. It was a decent plan, and that giant squid raised the hairs on my neck. Then Blackbeard smiled like he was honestly amused. "There are three flaws with your plan. One, I see your illusion. I spent the whole day learning about your technologies, and I'm a fast learner. That's no portal. That's what they call an Intelligent Telephone, correct? You can make it show me whatever you want it to. Doesn't mean it's real."

He walked around the three of us like a shark circling its prey, his sword pointed at us the whole time.

"Two, nobody tricks a pirate. We spend our lives being dishonest for profit. We can smell a trick leagues away."

He stopped in front of Wiki, putting his sword less than an inch from his nose.

"And three, Blackbeard fears nothing." He stopped for dramatic effect. "Now, you have three seconds to produce the bell or I'll have your head. Three. Two. One."

"You counted too fast!" I screamed. "I don't know how

pirates did it back then, but you're supposed to pause between each number—it builds tension!"

Blackbeard shrugged and raised his sword.

"We don't have the bell anymore!" Brady yelled. Blackbeard froze. "It's with Principal Gale now. It was waiting for her on her desk this morning, wrapped up extra nicely with a curly bow."

"What?!" the rest of us yelled at the same time. Brady smiled defiantly.

"You think I was going to trust my life to your plan when you had nothing by 8:00 p.m. last night?" She shook her head at Wiki and looked back at Blackbeard. "The bell is with your boss. Good luck trying to get it without ruining your cover at the school."

"Queen of Pirates," Blackbeard said through gritted teeth. But then he nodded approvingly. "Again, you impress me. I won't harm my future first mate, but here's a reminder not to cross me, ever—" He swung back his sword without warning, aiming his strike right for Wiki's neck.

I shut my eyes and was waiting for the worst, when we heard what sounded like an elephant crashing through the woods. I peeked one eye open. The elephant was getting closer. We could see the bushes and trees crashing around the beast, but we couldn't make out what it was. Blackbeard turned around, his eyes trying to follow the noise as it came closer, closer. Then, when it must have been just ten feet away, it stopped behind a huge tree next to us.

"The...Kraken?" Blackbeard whispered to himself. For a second I thought he might be right.

Then a shadow peeked out from the huge tree, impossible to see in the dark. Wait, not a shadow. *The* shadow.

"Mr. Teach," it said in woman's voice with a deep Caribbean accent, "perhaps I am seeing things, but it seems to me that you are threatening these three children."

Was Blackbeard getting nervous? Did I see sweat on his brow?

"These children are friends of the woods. Doing any harm to them would make the woods very angry. Were you going to hurt them? Were you going to anger the woods?"

Blackbeard mumbled, "Um, no. No m'lady, I was not."

"Wonderful, Mr. Teach. I thought not," the voice said, kindly but firmly. "Now please let us be. These friends of the forest no longer have what you seek."

Blackbeard awkwardly put his sword back in his belt and stomped out of the woods. "Oh, one more thing, Mr. Teach," the voice said as Blackbeard turned his head, not doing a good job of masking his anger. "The table will not listen to you. The table only listens to the Chosen Ones."

Blackbeard gave us a look, then stomped off. (Did she just call us the Chosen Ones?)

The shadow emerged from the tree. I held my breath, terrified at what the creature might look like in the light of day. My money was on glowing red eyes, a flaming skeleton for a body, and a mouth that sucked in people's souls. She took another step, then another, and then fully walked into the clearing with us. I shut my eyes until I could barely see out of them. But then I realized that the shadow's shape looked awfully familiar. I opened one eye fully.

Aunt Nancy?!

"Hello, my friends." She nodded casually, then

turned around and walked deeper into the woods. Our brains were so fried by her presence that we were frozen completely in place. She might as well have turned us to stone. We just watched her, hypnotized. After a few steps she turned to us.

"Coming?"

20

The three of us walked deeper into the woods
with Aunt Nancy, still too stunned to speak after what
just happened. It was getting darker and quieter as she
led us farther into a part of the woods I wasn't sure we'd
ever seen. The trees were taller and wider, and this part
of the forest seemed very old. And, as weird as it might
sound, kind of magical.

"Aunt Nancy? What? You? Here? Why?" Wiki couldn't
even put two words together. I didn't blame him. Neither
could I. Aunt Nancy just giggled to herself as she walked
a few feet in front of us.

"What Wiki means," Brady said, "is how did you find
us in the woods, how do you know about Mr. Teach,

and how in the blue blazes do you know about our table?"

Aunt Nancy seemed to ignore us, whistling happily to herself. Usually this would annoy Brady to the point of explosion, but we were all superfans of Wiki's aunt, and she was always this mysterious. She would talk when she wanted to talk. She always did eventually.

Finally we came to a clearing and we all sat down on the trunk of a massive fallen tree. "As you know, I am old friends with many teachers in your school." It was true. Wiki always got super embarrassed at parent night because Aunt Nancy would come too and schmooze it up with our teachers. "And you know I am always taking my afternoon walks in these woods. Well, it was lucky I ran into you during today's walk."

Everyone nodded, but I raised my hand. "Aunt Nancy? You didn't answer the million-dollar question. You know about the table, and you called us the Chosen Ones. How? And why?"

Her eyes twinkled. "First I must ask you a question. I believe it is my turn. Is mean Mr. Teach the only visitor you invited to dinner?"

"We invited three people total, but only Mr. Teach escaped," I said.

"Well, that is good news," she answered.

She stood up and walked over to a huge tree in front of us with long branches. Then she took a casual hop to the lowest branch. Except the lowest branch was almost ten feet in the air. It wasn't a completely impossible jump, but I'm guessing only people in the Olympics could have pulled that off. How old was Aunt Nancy anyway?

"As for your charming new table," she said, dangling her legs playfully from the branch, "his name is Brocéliandus."

So that's what all the scratched-out letters along his side spelled. I was going to stick with "Andy."

"His story is a long one. Full of tragedy. Full of adventure," she continued. "And it began not far from here, in a vast meadow in these very woods, when he was planted as the first tree in this forest. However, that is a tale for another day. What's important is that he had been missing for a very long time until now. Some thought he was hiding or sleeping, but it appears that you found him and woke him up! Now, he is a wise and wonderful spirit, but as you've proven, his powers can be very dangerous when misunderstood."

Wiki and I nodded, taking it in. (Magic tree. That would've been slightly cooler than a magic table.)

"It was wise of you to give the bell to the principal, Brady." Brady smiled, blushed, and curtsied. Wiki looked at her dubiously but then conceded. Brady's plan was better. "He is tricksy, that one," Aunt Nancy said as she looked in the direction of Finistere. "He charmed everyone else in that school, and they didn't suspect a thing. Of course, I knew better. No one is as tricksy as me." She was almost talking to herself. After a few seconds she turned back to look at us. "Don't worry about the pirate—he won't threaten you anymore."

"How did you spook one of the most fearless people in history?" I asked.

"Javi, everyone is afraid of the unknown. A forest like this is a scary place to a seafarer. I'm guessing he thinks I'm a forest witch." She chuckled.

"Well, what about the rest of the world?" Brady asked. "He's a threat to the entire planet, not just us."

Aunt Nancy shook her head kindly. "Ah, of course

you haven't realized this yet. This is important." She paused to make sure we were paying attention. "Anyone summoned by Andy may not leave the town. They are trapped within it. There is a wall around it that we can't see or feel, but they cannot venture past."

She must have seen the question in our eyes, because she went on: "The woods used to be much larger than they currently are. The school and the town surrounding it still have ancient trees lining them. Brocéliandus still considers that the woods."

She let us digest that for a second.

"How...how do you know all of this?" Wiki asked, looking at his aunt like she had ten heads.

Aunt Nancy smiled and shrugged. "I have lived in this town for a long time, Wiki. Much longer than your parents. Wander through the woods long enough and they begin to tell you their secrets. That is all. Now, I will talk with Gale about what happened here, and we will decide how to proceed."

Wait, what did she say? "Gale?" I asked. "As in, Principal Gale? What does she have to do with Andy?"

"Everything," Aunt Nancy said, and winked as she

hopped down from the branch and started walking deeper into the woods. After a few steps she turned around and bowed. "Apologies for the quick exit, but I need to go fix our dinner, Wiki. Follow the path ahead and it will lead you home. Good night, Javier. Good night, Brady. Wiki, see you soon." And with that she practically disappeared into the woods.

"Wait, I have a multitude of questions," Wiki called out, waving his hand. "How does a piece of furniture break the laws of temporal physics? Are Andy's purrs related to the summoning, and, if so, does that mean he's using vibrations to alter the space-time continuum? When these characters are sent back in time, are their memories erased, or do their memories from the future forever alter the past? Are you really my aunt?!"

The woods were silent for a second, then there was the familiar sound of an elephant crashing through the woods, except this time it was moving away from us. Then it was silent again.

"Nothing makes sense anymore," Brady said, looking intently into the woods. "Let's go home and talk this out."

"I don't know about you guys, but I could definitely use a grilled cheese right about now."

"Oh, we're not going home yet," Wiki said. "Follow me."

21

"**Everything... Everything... Everything...**"

Wiki had been muttering the same word over and over for the past hour like it was the sound of the engine in his brain.

We were deep in the high school library, huddled over a table that had books strewn all over it. Wiki was so lost in his head that he didn't explain why he was pulling out books that all seemed unrelated to each other, and not really related to anything that seemed important. When Wiki gets like this we mind our own business, so Brady was finishing her book on Blackbeard and I was copying recipes from cookbooks while I tried not to fall asleep.

Finally Brady finished her book, slammed it closed,

and walked up to Wiki, snapping her fingers in his face. "Okay, Wiki, wakey-wakey. We've been waiting patiently for approximately forever now, and these books are nonsense. What are you doing?"

He looked at her as if seeing her for the first time all day. "Brady. Oh, hi. This? This is a collection of books on temporal physics, quantum mechanics, and wormholes."

"I'm even more confused now, Brainiac."

Wiki looked over at us both. "I'm trying to piece together how Andy facilitates time travel. There has to be a mechanism. Then once I've solved that, we can move on to my aunt's strange behavior and her ominous statement about our principal."

"You're trying to solve time travel?" I asked, scratching my head. "I might not be a professional chef yet, but I'm pretty sure you've bitten off more than you can chew. Way more. Here's an idea: How about you park the time-travel thing, and we figure out what your aunt meant about Principal Gale."

"Everything," he repeated. "She has everything to do with Andy."

"Yeah, you've been saying 'everything' on loop since we got here. We heard her too." Brady sighed.

Mr. Bottom came walking over with a fat book. "Mr. Green, this massive tome is the most recent book on theoretical physics I could find." This was probably the twentieth book Mr. B had hunted down for Wiki in the last hour. "However, I don't recommend it—it's overly long and tedious. And brevity is the soul of wit."

"Hmmm, I think we're going to change the parameters of our search," Wiki said as he practically fell over from the weight of the book.

"Sorry," I said to Mr. B. "When he gets excited about something..."

"Ah, there's no need to apologize, Mr. Santiago. It is my greatest pleasure to help Mr. Green. He's the only student who makes full use of this library. Most students only request books in their curricula. Or on... Boi Squad." We all shuddered.

"Mr. Bottom, are there any books on the history of our school?" Wiki asked.

For a split second, Mr. B's eyes looked scared—or threatened. I doubt the others even noticed. He coughed awkwardly. "I don't believe so, no. There are articles about the school that would take me some time to find, but no book devoted to the school itself."

"How about books on the history of New Brittany?" he asked. "Probably in the local history section, 977.1, I would imagine?"

"We may have one or two, Mr. Green. This being a small town, they won't be very impressive, I'm afraid. Probably written by the local historical society. I will see what we have." Mr. B shuffled off into the depths of the library.

"That should at least be a good starting point," Wiki said, half to himself. "We'll see if there's anything in it that might lead us down a path to some answers."

"So Principal Gale has everything to do with Andy," I said as I tried to spin a book on my finger. "Maybe what Aunt Nancy means is that our principal used to be the Chosen One."

"Your point being?" Wiki asked.

"Well, it's like I said before: What if we weren't the only ones to use Andy? What if Principal Gale used him before?"

Brady started nodding, but Wiki shook his head.

"So what if Principal Gale had some really fancy dinner parties with historical figures?" he said. "I mean, it's fascinating, but it doesn't change anything. Like I said, if historical figures were running around in the modern world, we would absolutely know about it. And Andy would be locked up in some government laboratory getting studied by army scientists."

Mr. B showed up again holding a couple of books that looked stapled together. "Well, Mr. Green, it appears that we have one shoddy book hardly bigger than a pamphlet and another that looks like somebody's stapled-together homework," he said. "Hardly worth studying, but here they are." He handed them to Wiki, who looked pretty disappointed. "Pipe up if your curiosity sets you down a different path," Mr. B added as he walked back to the front desk.

Wiki sat down to look at the books, and I kept thinking about my theory as I walked aimlessly down the rows of bookshelves.

It did make some sense. If Gale was Andy's Chosen One for a while, she probably invited some awesome people to dinner over the years. I bet she became friends with some of them and invited them over many times. Kind of like Kid Mozart. If we got the bell back I was definitely going to invite him over again. But I wonder if Gale ever invited them to live in our world permanently? That seemed kind of irresponsible, and she's anything but that. Still... maybe she could disguise them really well.

Wait, where was I? I snapped out of my daydream because it had gotten so dark. I was definitely deep in the maze of shelves, but I'd ended up somewhere where there was almost zero light. I could barely read the book titles right in front of my face. Then I looked up and realized I couldn't see to the top of the shelves. For some reason that spooked me out enough that I shivered. I kept looking up, squinting my eyes to see if maybe I could make out the top of the shelves, but they seemed to go into infinity. Then I caught a glint of something high up. Way high up. Too high up, I thought. But it glinted again. Something was up there.

I could have ignored it. I could have asked Mr. B what it was. I could have tried sneaking his ladder over here. I could have even called out to Wiki or Brady for some help. But nope, in that moment, I thought the smartest thing to do was climb up the infinite-looking shelves to see what was up there. If you could get graded on decisions, I would've gotten an F+.

So I started climbing. It wasn't hard at first. I used to climb up a couple of shelves at the middle school library to reach cookbooks when no librarians were looking. That was easy peasy. But after I got to the sixth or seventh shelf here, I noticed that I couldn't see the ground. And it felt like I was looking down into a bottomless pit. I gripped the shelf so tightly my knuckles turned white, and I tried to stop my heart from beating so hard and fast that my chest felt like a punching bag. No dice. Keep moving, Javi. I started the climb again, forcing myself to look up, not down.

At this point I felt like I was floating in space. I couldn't see the floor below or the end of the shelves above. There was nothing to do but climb. Shelf. Shelf. Shelf. Shelf. At some point I'd lost count. Was I on the twentieth shelf? Twenty-fifth? The only thing I knew for sure was that if I slipped, that was it for me—game over, adios, life. Why did I decide to do this again?

The thing glinting above me was finally getting closer. Ten shelves away. Five. Two. One. Finally this thing was within reach. I'd risked my life for whatever it was. A sword? A jet pack? A robot butler to do my every bidding? I reached over and felt for it. Metallic. Smooth. Small. It was a...lock? I wiggled it and it opened. Hmmm, a locked shelf in a mysterious library. It was no Excalibur, but it was still kind of cool.

I held on for dear life with one hand and slid open the wooden door to the shelf. Then I peered inside. It was...books. Of course it was. I could barely make out any of their titles, but none of the ones I could read seemed all that interesting. They seemed like biographies, mostly. They were also packed in extra tight. I tried pulling out a tall, thin book, but it was harder than it looked. I had to stabilize myself with one hand, plant my feet firmly on the lower shelf, and pull with my whole body. The book slid out slowly, an inch at a time. Come on...come on...

Then, all at once, the book practically flew off the shelf and out of my hands. It dropped into the bottomless pit below me for what seemed like a full minute. And then

I heard a thunderous SLAM! Oh no. I bet people in New York heard that sound.

"Is everything all right?" I heard Mr. B say from far away. This was not cool at all. Could kids go to jail? If so, I was definitely heading straight there. Do not pass Go, Javi. Do not collect $200.

I was so scared of Mr. B catching me that I skittered down the shelves like a spider, not once thinking that I was one slip away from death. *Hurry, Javi, hurry.* I climbed down so fast I didn't even count the shelves by ones, I counted by fives until I lost track. Just as I started to wonder if the shelves were magical and never ending, my feet hit floor. Oh floor, blessed floor! I was about to kiss it with joy.

Then I looked down at the book that had fallen. It was titled *Frida Kahlo: Mexico's Greatest Painter*. And the woman on the cover was Ms. Calderon.

22

"**You are absolutely, 100 percent, completely** out of your mind if you don't see it."

"For the nine-hundredth time, Javi, she does look similar, but there are plenty of normal folks who look like famous artists."

"For being a genius, you can be pretty dumb sometimes," I shot back. "And as bullheaded as...well, as a bull."

I wasn't super happy with Wiki. It was Saturday, and I couldn't believe we were still having this conversation a day later. When I showed him my big discovery in the library—the one I risked my life for—he just shrugged and said it was a funny coincidence. Brady freaked out, as she should have, but Wiki spent the next three hours arguing that there was no way our art teacher was an Andy-summoned famous artist from almost a hundred years ago. So I swallowed my anger and told him to come over the next day.

Now he still wasn't buying it, and that was after:

- We flipped through the book's pages and looked at dozens of paintings and photos that were clearly one hundred percent Ms. C—same big, long eyebrows, same intense look—even the faces she made and the way she smiled were pure Ms. C.
- I did some research and noticed that Frida Kahlo's birth name was Magdalena Carmen Frida Kahlo y Calderón. Duh, her alias was her birth name!
- In one painting she was hanging out with her dog—the same dog she brought to class on Bring Your Pet to School Day.

Then I'd pulled out our yearbook to cross-reference Ms. C's photos with Frida Kahlo's. They were absolutely the same person, but Wiki just kept shaking his head. If it wasn't plainly obvious before, Wiki is as stubborn as a hundred mules, and it's by far the most annoying thing about him.

"Look, just because you didn't figure this out first, doesn't mean it's not true. What proof do you need to believe me? Do you need her to tell you herself?"

"Okay, Javi, let's pretend I agreed with you. So what if she's Frida Kahlo? So Principal Gale made a dinner party friend and let her teach here for a while. Big deal. Nobody else would ever believe us if we told them, anyway."

"Do I have to spell it out for you?" I asked him, fully exasperated. "Look, I didn't just pull out this yearbook to show you Ms. Kahlo. I pulled it out because I bet there are other teachers that Andy summoned and are teaching at Finistere. That locked cabinet in the library had a bunch of books in it, and I doubt they were all about Frida Kahlo."

Wiki gave me a dubious look. I ignored him.

"But I need your help," I continued. "I don't recognize any of these last names, but I don't know nearly as many historic people as you do. Can you just look through the yearbook and tell me if any of these could be from history?"

"You honestly think there are more people from history teaching here? Well, first of all, you're wrong. But secondly, on the very slim chance that there's another one, they would also use an alias like Ms. C, so we wouldn't know."

I glared at him and shoved the yearbook in his face. He groaned and flipped through it quietly, studying every teacher's name and picture. Now that it was a puzzle that would prove his smarts, he was a little more into it.

"Nope, nope, nope." He repeated that word about a hundred times, then handed the yearbook back to me. "Andy didn't summon any teachers from history."

"Or, like you said, Gale's just good at giving them an alias so parents don't suspect."

"Or you're just letting your imagination run wild. And Ms. Calderon just happens to look like a famous artist."

"Javi," Brady called from downstairs. "It's dinner-time. Wiki, are you still being a stubborn jerk?"

Wiki rolled his eyes. "Let's eat." We walked downstairs and into the kitchen, where Brady was waiting for us.

"Did he convince you that he's right?" she asked Wiki as she put plates on the table. "Just because Javi's never right doesn't mean he can't be right now."

"Um...thanks?" I said. Was that even a compliment?

"You know what, Wiki?" she said. "Just ask Aunt Nancy and be done with it. She knew all about Andy, I bet she'd know about the teachers."

Wiki shook his head. "Aunt Nancy's not saying a word about anything Andy-related. You know how she can be." Then he pointed at us. "Now, let's focus on the actual danger we're in. There's still a murderous pirate who wants the four of us dead. And I'm still at a loss about how to stop him."

"I don't know..." Brady said. "Did you see the way Blackbeard looked at us when Aunt Nancy told him he couldn't use the bell? He believed her. Plus, now he knows we don't have it, and he's not going to mess with Principal Gale. He's probably coming up with a new plan. I think we're safe. At least for now."

"We're not safe until Blackbeard's gone," Wiki replied flatly.

"Hold on. Rewind," I said, my finger firmly planted in

Wiki's chest. "Did you just say he wants four of us dead? I count three of us. I've always counted three. Wait...do you still count Betty the Yeti?" Brady glared at me for bringing up her old imaginary friend.

Wiki took a step toward Andy and knocked his knuckles on the table. "Number four." We gasped, and he looked disappointed in us. "Didn't you hear what my aunt said? Blackbeard's trapped in the woods right now because of Andy's magic. Once he invites his crew into our world he has no use for Andy. So adios, table."

Brady's eyes narrowed to slits. "Over my dead body."

Wiki nodded his head glumly. "I think that's his intention, yeah. So tomorrow I'm taking the day to see if I can cobble together a better plan than the last one and save us. All four of us."

"If you want to waste the day, go nuts," Brady said. "We are 100 percent safe while Gale has that bell. Trust me."

"Brady's right," I said. "It feels like we've been holding our breath for days. Why not just exhale for a minute? We still need to get rid of the pirate, but he's no threat right this second."

Dad came into the kitchen and we had dinner. He

spent the whole meal cracking jokes at Wiki, but Wiki was too stressed to laugh. Brady kept petting Andy firmly like he was a frightened kitten, whispering the same thing over and over again: "Over my dead body."

23

It was almost midnight when I heard them.
There must have been at least twenty people gathering
on our doorstep, chanting something that sounded like,
"Assault! Assault!" It took me a second to realize I wasn't
dreaming, and when I did, I shot up and looked around
frantically. Wiki and I had conked out in the living
room while watching old monster movies. The TV was
off, it was basically pitch black, and the chanting was
getting louder and louder. Blackbeard? Did he somehow
summon his pirates? So this was it—our worst nightmare was actually happening! It was all over.

My dad came rushing down the stairs and when
he opened the door, people came flooding into the

living room screaming. I froze as twenty shadows surrounded us, every one of them holding something different in their hands that I couldn't quite make out. For a second it was quiet, until one of them shouted, "Now! Ahora!" and as someone flicked the lights on, they all began to scream.

No, not exactly scream—more like singing. Really loud singing. With instruments. They were all holding instruments.

Wiki shot up shrieking, "Blackbeard! Pirates! We're done for!"

And then I started laughing.

See, this is actually a totally normal thing that happens to Puerto Rican houses from time to time. These weren't pirates—they were Dad's friends. This was a parranda.

You know how during the holidays Christmas carolers will ring your doorbell, sing you a song or two, and then leave? Yeah, the Puerto Rican version of Christmas caroling is way more intense.

It's called a parranda and also an asalto (assault). A bunch of friends get together with instruments, and once it's nice and late, and most normal people are sleeping, they head to a friend's or neighbor's house, bang on their door, and wake them up with their preposterously loud singing.

Now here's where it gets wild. As a Puerto Rican, you aren't allowed to be mad, or to go back to sleep, or keep your door shut. You have to let them in, feed them all, sing with them, and then join them as they go to the next house to do the exact same thing. As it gets later and later, the group of people in a parranda grows and grows and they raid friends' pantries and fridges and basically eat all the food at house after house after house, getting louder and louder after every one. Sometimes until four in the morning. Oh, and here in New Brittany the Puerto Ricans love parrandas so much they do them year-round.

All of this might sound awful, and it might sound completely bonkers, but I actually love it. And hey, it meant that we weren't about to get sliced and diced in the comfort of our living room, so that was a plus.

"Javi, feed us!" some of the people shouted at me between songs. "We're starving!"

"Do you know these people?" Wiki yelped as he put on his glasses to get a better look at the chaos around us. "Because we should call the cops!"

"These are Dad's friends," I said as I jumped out of my sleeping bag, high-fived some of the folks who were there, and headed to the kitchen. Dad's crew loves to come parranda at our house because they know I make all the best food.

I opened the fridge to take stock of what I could feed them. Dad's amigos were in luck—I'd made a kingly feast a few days ago, and there were plenty of leftovers. When I closed the fridge to pull out some plates, Aunt Nancy was sitting on the kitchen counter recovering from a laugh attack.

"Did you see his face, Javi? Did you see Wiki's face? Oh, that was so very worth it." Aunt Nancy never missed a parranda, because nothing makes her happier than a good prank. Reason #9,629 that she's the best adult ever.

"I honestly thought his head was going to explode." I chuckled. "But I kinda thought mine would too."

"You three have seemed so stressed lately, you could use a little fun. Especially after the incident in the woods," she said. I nodded heavy nods. She wasn't wrong. "Now, tell me how you want me to help. I'll be your sous-chef. What's on the menu?"

In no time, the two of us were heating up plates and putting them on Andy, calling out each dish as we did. Soon there must have been thirty people crammed into our dining room and singing at the top of their lungs as they stuffed their faces. Meanwhile we got to work on jibarito sandwiches, a sandwich superior to all other sandwiches because instead of bread, you use—wait for it...TOSTONES. Yeah, double-fried plantains as a bun with meat, lettuce, tomato, and mayo inside. If great food made heads explode, this would bomb your brains.

"Don't these people understand the nature of circadian rhythms?" Wiki moaned as Aunt Nancy and I flipped tostones. "It's detrimental to one's health to be awoken and roused at this time of night. The music alone will make sleep nearly impossible for hours afterward."

"Eat, Wiki! Before it's all gone," Dad said as he walked by. "The shrimp that falls asleep gets taken by the current." Wiki raised an eyebrow—huh? Aunt Nancy winked at Dad and they laughed.

"Here, help me carry this," I said to Wiki as he made a face at me. Between the two of us we heaved out the mammoth plate of sandwiches and laid it in the middle of Andy, who must have been sagging under the weight of all the food plus two guys with guitars sitting on him as they led the sing-alongs.

I headed back to the semi-quiet kitchen to clean up some of the mess. Aunt Nancy was already washing the pans, humming a Caribbean song to herself, and smiling that trademark wicked smile as she did a little dance. When she saw me she clapped loudly. "Javier Santiago, the hero of the parranda! Three cheers for the hero!"

Hero. I was hardly a hero. Wait...a hero! It hit me like a ton of bricks. No, harder than that. It hit me like a giant dump truck carrying ten tons of bricks, driven by two extra-chunky hippos. "How else do you face the baddest bad guy of all time? With the bestest good guy of all time!" I whispered to myself. I hugged a surprised Aunt Nancy and raced out of the kitchen to find Wiki and Brady.

"Okay, guys, I've got it. The way we defeat the pirate." I'd dragged them up to my room to explain my plan.

"Think about it. You keep saying that Beardo is the worst villain of all time. Well, I've read enough comics to know that the only surefire way to defeat an epic villain is with an epic hero." I smiled triumphantly, but they both looked annoyed.

"Summon a hero? Javi, I literally had that idea the day after we summoned Blackbeard," Brady said. "Wiki shot it down because he thinks summoning anyone else is the worst idea." Wiki nodded at Brady, then rolled his eyes at me. "That's why I gave the bell to the principal."

"You don't get it," I said. "Guys, if Principal Gale summoned Frida Kahlo, then I'm sure there are other historical folks at our school. And I bet there's someone there who can face Freakbeard and win. We just need to find them."

Wiki curled his hands slowly into fists in front of his face, his favorite thing to do when he was super frustrated. "Javi, enough is enough. For the last time, there aren't famous knights and samurai warriors and heroes of yore wandering the halls of Finistere. Ms. Calderon isn't Frida Kahlo. In fact, if you mention Frida Kahlo one more time, my head will actually explode."

CRASH! Something heavy shattered on the dining room floor. We all gasped, then peeked out of my room to see shattered glass. Dad's favorite vase.

The music stopped instantly, and everyone got really quiet. As wild as parrandas can get, you're not supposed to actually destroy someone's house at one. Dad's friends all looked over at him. For a good five seconds he stared at the shattered glass, horrified. Then he looked up at his buddies and...shrugged?

"On to the next house!" someone said. "Vamonos, amigos! Asalto! Asalto!"

His friends all cheered, and they paraded out of the house singing at the top of their lungs. My dad waved to them from the door, explaining that he couldn't just abandon his kids in the middle of the night. Before he shut it he turned to the three of us. "You guys are good sports."

Wiki practically followed them out, shaking his head at me the whole way. "Don't talk to me tomorrow. One of us has to come up with a viable plan."

I don't know how late we went to bed, but I hibernated all of Sunday. I spent the entire day cross-referencing my yearbook with Dad's encyclopedias, hoping for a face to match. It was a supremely dumb and pointless activity, but it helped me completely forget about the madness awaiting us at school.

24

Monday was the Mondayest Monday of all Mondays. Not only was Wiki mad at himself for not hatching a plan over the weekend, but he spent the entire walk to Finistere scolding us for being too relaxed about Blackbeard. "We need to face the school bully before it's too late—except our bully is bearded, legendary, and very capable of murder," he ranted. "And it might be too late already." We just gave him the silent treatment. I was still pretty annoyed with him for being so hardheaded about the whole Ms. C situation.

I was about to walk into first-period science when Wiki stopped and pointed to a sign on the door. Scrimshaw Science across the hall—room 108. "Looks

like Mr. Jekyll is subbing for Mr. Scrimshaw today."
Mr. Jekyll had been our science teacher last year.
"Ooh, wait. Jekyll? A scientist? And he's British. What
if he's secretly *Doctor* Jekyll?" Wiki chuckled. Then
full-on laughed. Then had a mini laugh attack. "Can
you imagine if your absurd theory was actually right?
That'd be apocalyptic!"

I got a little excited and a lot confused. "Dr. Jekyll. Is
that a famous guy from history?"

"No," he laughed, drying his eyes as he walked past
me to his class. "It's doubly impossible because he's
not from history. Dr. Jekyll's a character in a book. But
he's the absolute last person you want in the real world.
Good thing you're completely wrong about all of this."
Then he walked off to his first-period class.

I walked into the room even more annoyed at Wiki, if
that were possible at this point.

"Good afternoon, children. Today we're going to take
a break from marine biology to conduct a quick yet
fascinating chemistry experiment involving selenium
and zirconium. Please procure your notebooks and we
shall begin." I'd forgotten how boring Mr. Jekyll's class

was unless you were super into science experiments. He spoke like a British butler from olden times, he got really excited about mixing liquids that were different colors, and he loved sounding out the names of chemicals that were ridiculously long and complicated. So, yeah, Wiki used to absolutely love his class. Me? Not so much.

"Now, let us begin with selenium. Pencils are out? Good." As he droned on I thought about what Wiki had said. So, clearly Andy summoned people from history, but what if he summoned people from fiction too? If Wiki were here he'd probably say something about time travel at least being theoretically possible but fiction just being made-up garbage. But Wiki wasn't here, and I was desperate for a lead. Why not at least look into it?

Once Mr. J finished lecturing and we started doing our lab, I faked having to look something up on the computer. "It'll just take a minute, Mr. Jekyll. I'm really interested in millennium."

"Selenium," he corrected.

"Uh, yeah, that too. One sec."

The computers faced the classroom, so as I researched Dr. Jekyll online, I was pretty terrified that Mr. Jekyll would notice. Especially once I started reading about him. The fictional Dr. Jekyll was a normal scientist who made a potion that would turn him into a monster called Hyde whenever he wanted, but after a while the monster started taking over, and Jekyll had no control of the transformations—he would randomly turn into Hyde. Now I could see why Wiki was making fun of me. Pirates and earls were one thing, but summoning monsters from books was another thing completely.

But then I read Jekyll's description from the book: "A large, well-made, smooth-faced man of fifty." Yep, that was Mr. Jekyll to a tee. "Every mark of capacity and kindness." If "capacity" meant smarts, then yeah, Mr. Jekyll was both really smart and super nice. Boring, but nice. Then I read some quotes that Jekyll says in the book, and...oh boy. He talked exactly like Mr. Jekyll.

"Almost done there, chap?" Jekyll asked. I almost peed myself, but instead I quickly shut the computer off, jumped out of my seat, and scrambled to the lab tables.

"Done, done, done," I said. Whew—it looked like he hadn't noticed what I was researching.

That's when I got another stupendously dumb idea

in my head. What if I tested Mr. Jekyll out to see if there was a Mr. Hyde lurking in there? If there really was, I bet we could set him off in class. But of course there wouldn't be, so there was really zero danger. You know how they say curiosity killed the cat? Well, I bet curiosity completely slaughters the Javi one day.

"Hey, Grimes," I whispered. "Code Red."

Grimes gave me a cruel look. "Is that a challenge, Santiago? Because if so, I accept."

Code Red wasn't something you said lightly. It was like a missile-launch code. It triggered the class to go completely haywire. We only used it on really bad or boring substitute teachers. As far as I knew, no one had ever tried a Code Red on a nice sub. But in seconds Grimes had walked to every kid in the class and whispered "Code Red" in their ear. Some of them shook their heads—Code Red on sweet, innocent Mr. J? But enough of them were bored or brave enough that they nodded.

"Hmmmmmmmmmmmmmmm..."

It came from behind me. It was Sarah. Oh boy. Secret Crush Sarah was getting in on it.

"What in the blazes is that noise?" Mr. Jekyll said, looking back from the chalkboard. "Is that one of you?"

The loud hum continued. Mr. Jekyll started looking around the room, trying to pinpoint where it was coming from. Just as he started zeroing in on Sarah, the hum started coming from another direction. For a surprisingly long time he stood silent, trying to follow the sound, getting more annoyed every second.

"Is it you? Which of you is it? Enough!"

The humming prank. It brings down even the calmest teachers. Sure, it only works when the entire class is in on it and one student can pick up when another student stops, but when it does work, it's true torture. I already regretted my decision. Poor, innocent Mr. J. What was I thinking?

"Hmmmmmmmmmmmmmmmm..."

Jekyll pinched the bridge of his nose, inhaled, and then exhaled slowly. I could swear I saw his pinkie twitching a little bit. "Please do not continue to test my patience, students. I assure you, you do not want to make me angry."

If there was a monster in there, we were probably close to unleashing it. Too late to stop now.

That's when Grimes whispered "Launch!" and an armada of paper airplanes began. One after the other they flew, from all different corners of the room, each one crashing into Jekyll's face, or arms, or, in one case, getting stuck between his glasses and his eyes. At first he was surprised, then one or two looked like they actually stung him, and for the first time I saw his usual pleasant smile turn into a scowl.

"What has gotten into you children?" he said, done with being irritable and now downright angry. His eyes twitched as he picked paper airplanes off the floor, crumpling each one up. "Is this how you treat a professor? What abominations you are today!"

Okay, that should've done it. No monster. So Andy just plucked people from history—no talking animals or dragons from books get summoned into our world. Double whew.

Argh, I felt awful for what I just did to the boring-but-otherwise-nice Mr. J. Maybe I could explain my dumb idea to him later and he would semi-forgive me? Or send me to the nurse thinking I'd gone insane?

"Mr. J! Mr. J!" Grimes yelled, waving his hand in the air.

"Yes, Mr. Grimes?" Jekyll said, not happy about being interrupted.

"I really, really need to go to the bathroom."

Jekyll ran an angry hand through his hair. "You couldn't be bothered to wait until I finished speaking?"

"I just have to go really super bad. Like, it's practically coming out."

Jekyll winced. "Fine. Take the pass."

Grimes strutted to the front of the class and grabbed the bathroom pass that was attached to a big peacock feather, holding the pass with one hand and the feather with the other. Jekyll began to address the class again, when he was immediately interrupted again.

"Lighten up, Mr. J!" Grimes lunged at Mr. Jekyll and started tickling him with the huge feather. At first Mr. Jekyll was shocked, and then, for a little while, he started giggling uncontrollably, which was pretty hilarious. But then I started to notices flashes of anger, and then even scarier, flashes of fear. Why was he scared? "Not the tickling! Anything...but...the tickling!" he yelled between gasps.

No one else seemed to notice, but one of Jekyll's

hands was now three times the size of the other one, and it was extra hairy and looked more like concrete than skin. Oh. No. This guy is one hundred percent monster. *Abort! Abort!*

"Grimes! *RUN!*" I yelled, jumping out of my chair.

But it was too late. It felt like slow motion. Jekyll's laughter started sounding deeper and more like an animal's, but the class kept laughing hysterically. Grimes then turned around and bowed.

Then it happened. It actually happened. All at once the meek teacher's body started convulsing and transforming. First his other hand swelled up to three times its size, then his chest and torso ripped his shirt and suit jacket as it ballooned into a ginormous, monster-sized body, his legs ripping his pants as they caught up with the rest. Then, finally, the scariest part—his head went from being quiet old Mr. J to turning into something hideous and troll-like with huge, nasty features, tusks growing out of his teeth, and eyes that were blood red.

No. Way.

I couldn't move. I was completely frozen in place. My eyes were probably bigger than my entire face at that point. A lot of us were stunned, but the screams also came immediately.

"We're in a horror movie! Let's get out of here!"

"More like a comic book! Run, run, run!"

"What the—? Mommy!"

Mr. Hyde turned slowly to face us, smiling hideously as he spoke in a deep, thunderous growl that gave me goosebumps.

"I'M FREE AGAIN! A++ TO WHOEVER UNLEASHED ME FROM MY PUNY CAGE!" he said, ripping the teacher's desk from the floor and throwing it out the window like it weighed five pounds. "I FEEL GREAT! NOW LET'S GET THIS PARTY STARTED!" he yelled, punching a huge hole in the wall for fun. "MUSIC!" He looked at the class expectantly, but everyone was frozen in their seats and probably peeing themselves. "I SAID...MUSIC!"

Tommy in the front row woke up from his shock, plugged his phone into the class stereo, and pushed play.

"THAT'S MORE LIKE IT! NOW I GO BOOM AND YOU GO CLAP. BOOM!" he growled as he punched a hole in the ceiling. It took us a second, but a few kids clapped.

"ALL OF YOU, AGAIN. BOOM!" Now he head-butted an empty desk, breaking it in half. More kids clapped, but a lot of them were still in shock. "TO THE RHYTHM, PEOPLE! BOOM!" He cracked a huge glass beaker on his head. A few of the wilder kids started getting into it, clapping loudly.

"This dude is rad!" Grimes said. "Let's do this, guys— boom, clap, boom, clap!"

"THAT'S THE SPIRIT!" Mr. Hyde growled happily as he pointed at Grimes. Now the class started clapping more and more enthusiastically as Hyde danced around the room, smashing desks, throwing chairs out the windows, doing a cannonball into a table as it practically exploded, and head-butting just about everything else, all to the beat.

"Best science class ever!" Grimes shouted.

"IT SURE IS! NOW START THROWING STUFF AT ME!" he thundered, pointing eagerly at his open mouth. Most of the kids were too afraid to, but without missing a beat, Grimes tossed a huge glass cylinder at his head, and Hyde caught it with his mouth, cracking the glass with his teeth and swallowing it.

"Go Mr. J!" Sarah yelled.

"CALL ME HYDE!" he roared as someone else threw a globe at him, which he chomped and swallowed.

"Hyde! Hyde! Hyde! Hyde!" the class started chanting.

"WOO! I FEEL GOOD! DO YOU FEEL GOOD?"

"Yes!" the class shouted.

"I FEEL SO GOOD I WANT TO PUNCH SOMEONE IN THE FACE! WHO WANTS TO GET PUNCHED IN THE FACE?" Hyde said, in a surprisingly friendly tone, like he'd just asked us who wanted to get ice cream with him.

The whole class now went immediately silent as Hyde looked around excitedly, one fist cocked back and ready to punch.

"NO ONE? AW, COME ON!"

A lot of the kids backed away and tried to fade into the wall at the other end of the classroom.

"YOU GUYS DON'T KNOW HOW TO PARTY! OH WELL, I'LL FIND SOMEONE WHO DOES!" And with that Hyde took a running start and leapt through the wall with the windows, leaving a huge, gaping hole behind.

The whole class ran to the hole and watched as Hyde did cartwheels and somersaults all the way to the edge of the forest. Right before he leapt into the woods he turned around, looked at our class through the huge hole in the wall, and made a dramatic bow. Then he backflipped into the woods with a huge roar.

There was a moment of complete silence after he disappeared. Then half the class reacted like they'd just seen a monster (which they had) and started crying or just staring at the floor in terror, while the other half reacted like they'd just chugged ten coffees in a row.

"Hyde for principal!" Grimes yelled, doing cartwheels around the room.

"Hyde for president!" Sarah corrected him, throwing beakers and test tubes at the wall and watching them shatter with delight.

That half of the class was dancing, doing headstands, or else just breaking stuff. But that only lasted for a few seconds, because soon the other teachers started pouring into the room.

"What in blue heaven happened here?!" a math teacher asked, practically fainting.

But half the class had already started chanting again.

"Hyde! Hyde! Hyde! Hyde!"

It was a while until things calmed down.

25

The afternoon was definitely interesting.
First the teachers tried getting a straight story out of the
class, but they didn't love what we were saying. (I mean,
how would you react to "Our science teacher turned
into an insane monster and wrecked the class to music
while we cheered"?) Then the cops showed up and tried
getting a more believable story out of us, but they didn't
do any better.

I'm not sure how it would have ended if Mr. Jekyll
hadn't stumbled out of the forest a few hours later, his
clothes in tatters. A teacher spotted him at the edge of
the woods and ran toward him, the cops following. They
gave him a lab coat, brought him to the classroom, and

half of our class looked at him in horror while the other half tried to high-five him. "Bring back Hyde! Bring back Hyde!" they started chanting until the cops shut them up.

Jekyll told a different story—of course he did—which made him sound like the victim. According to him, some crazy, super-strong guy wandered into the class and attacked him. He tried defending the class, but the guy chased him into the woods. Jekyll eventually lost him, but the guy must have been wandering the woods somewhere.

"How do you explain the hole?" the cop in charge asked, pointing to the wall.

"It must have been an unfortunate chemical reaction—perhaps he knocked the Berthelot's salt into the red phosphorous. I'm just so happy that the children are safe," he said. Honestly, that part sounded sincere. Maybe Jekyll didn't have much control over this Hyde guy. And maybe he wasn't on good terms with him either.

Things were starting to get a bit calmer now that the cops and teachers seemed to be buying Jekyll's story.

I had been in full freak-out mode since it happened. I mean, Hyde seemed friendly, but he also seemed super excited about punching people in the face. And his fists were bigger than my head.

Well, to be fair, Wiki would probably think up a foolproof plan that would save us from getting Hyded to death. Now that it had been a few hours, I was starting to breathe normally again.

Then who waltzed into our classroom but one Edward Teach.

Blackbeard took a look around the room, asked a student what happened, and then nodded thoughtfully. The cops might not be buying our story, but someone who had just traveled through time thanks to a magic table probably would. As the cops and teachers dispersed, Blackbeard walked over to Jekyll and put out his hand. "Edward Teach," he said excitedly, as they shook hands. He then put his arm around Jekyll and walked him out the door. "You and I have a lot to talk about, my new friend..." He turned his head as he walked out the door, made eye contact with me, and gave a devilish smile. Gulp.

———

"What about a dumpling?" I asked Wiki and Brady.

The three of us had just been called down to Principal Gale's office. After she asked us to take a seat, she told us to give her a minute and left the room again. I knew she was going to grill me about Jekyll and Hyde, so I didn't want to tell the story twice. I was trying to make small talk, but...yeah, I'm the worst at small talk.

"It's meat or veggies surrounded by dough. I mean, it's basically fillings sandwiched between a kind of bread. I think that's definitely a sandwich. You've gotta give me that one."

"Javi, would you just tell us what happened already?" Brady blurted out. "You don't think we heard the huge crash earlier? Or noticed a gaping hole in the science class as we walked by? Or saw all the cops that are walking the halls? The teachers aren't saying anything yet, but we know you were in there."

Wiki was pacing the room, breathing into a paper bag, and talking to himself—clearly he was about to completely lose his mind. "It's impossible. It's completely and utterly impossible. That book is fiction.

No part of that story is real. Dr. Jekyll isn't based on a real character. And nobody—no actual human—transforms into a monster."

I scrunched all the muscles in my face, looked at Brady, and managed to give the tiniest nod. "It's possible."

"Whoa. What's he like?" Brady asked.

"Hmmm. Well, you know how there's all those different versions of *Beauty and the Beast,* and in some versions the Beast looks awesome and kind of nice but in others he looks like a terrifying monster that would probably make you poop your pants if you ever saw him in real life? Yeah, Hyde is like the poop-your-pants version. He's huge, he has tusks for teeth, he could probably fit your whole body into his hand and then crunch all the bones and—"

"Enough! Okay, okay, I get it. Ew. I'm freaked out enough as it is."

Wiki kept pacing and talking to himself. "Have my parents written out my will? Because they must. Tonight. I'm as good as dead. A pirate teaming up with a monster—they should write out their wills too. Everybody should. We're all dead." He breathed into his bag again.

"That's not true," said Principal Gale's voice behind us. She walked in with Ms. Calderon and Mr. Scrimshaw, who closed the door as Gale sat at her desk in front of us. Ms. Calderon and Mr. Scrimshaw took their places standing on either side of her. Okay, that was weird...

"First things first. Javi, are you okay? Did he hurt you or anyone in the class?" Principal Gale asked.

"No, he didn't touch anyone. He broke a bunch of desks and ate glass and tore a huge hole in a brick wall, but no one was hurt."

Wiki's jaw dropped.

"At least no one was hurt. Now, it appears that you might have known more about Mr. Teach than you let on when we last met." Gale held up the bell and I gulped audibly. "Don't worry, I understand why you might have been hesitant to say anything, given the circumstances."

She scooted her chair closer to the desk, put her clasped hands on it, and looked at each of us carefully. "Now that we are all on the same page, it is important that you tell me the complete story. Please be honest, and don't leave anything vital out. Don't worry if some of it sounds impossible or made up. We know what Brocéliandus is capable of."

We?

"The whole story..." I muttered, staring at her emerald necklace because I couldn't look her in the eyes. "I'm trying to figure out where to even begin."

"Well, where did you meet Brocéliandus? That's a good place to start."

I inhaled once, gathered my thoughts, and began. I told her about finding him in the antique store, our assignment, our dinner party, and everything after. Wiki and Brady jumped in with details, and Brady even made sound effects at crucial moments. The entire time I talked, the three adults looked at us intently. I could tell they were working things out in their heads, and I could tell that this definitely wasn't the first time someone had been summoned by Andy.

When I was finished, Gale looked down at the desk, deep in thought. After some time she looked back up at us.

"So 16 Fig Tree Road is the new gateway."

"Excuse me?" Wiki said. "Did you call their house a gateway?"

"Yes," she said, looking at Wiki. "It is clear that Brocéliandus chose you three, and that until he decides otherwise, Javi and Brady's house is the gateway."

"A gateway to what, exactly?" I asked.

"Not to, from. A gateway from just about anywhere. It seems to be limited only by one's imagination. Set the place cards on the table, ring the bell and—snap!—any guest appears." She then gave us a little smile. "We are lucky that you are the Chosen Ones. Brocéliandus has been missing for a very long time, and we've been afraid someone less ethical would awaken him. It happened before, and it caused a lot of...problems. But that is a story for another time. Let us get through our present challenge first, as it is not insignificant."

Just as she was getting to the good stuff.

"So you understand the secret of Finistere now, lads," Mr. Scrimshaw said.

"And it is very important that you keep it a secret," Ms. Calderon added, looking at us sternly.

Brady tilted her head and looked at them. "Wait, was

Javi actually right? Is Finistere's secret that it's hiding Jekyll and you, Ms. Calderon? I mean, Ms. Kahlo."

Ms. Kahlo smiled, and Brady glared at Wiki. "See? Javi can be right once in his life." I blushed.

Gale stood up, walked around her desk, and sat on it, looking at us seriously. "You have trusted me with your important secret, so I will trust you with mine. The secret of Finistere isn't just about Ms. Kahlo or Mr. Jekyll. It's much bigger than that. It's about the school's mission."

"And what exactly is that?" Wiki asked, leaning forward. Gale was speaking his language.

"Finistere's mission is to be the single best school in the world."

She walked over to a framed picture of the faculty and pointed to it. "The quality of a school isn't in the building or the curriculum or the facilities. It's entirely in the faculty. Great teachers make for a great school. So we find and hire the very best teachers out there for this school."

She walked back to her desk and sat down. "Now, the best teachers don't all live in Maryland. And they're not all alive at this moment in history. And some of them exist in other worlds entirely. But I am gathering them here because I can. Because of Brocéliandus. Who is a better art teacher than Frida Kahlo? And who knows more about science than Dr. Jekyll? And there are a few others."

Scrimshaw chuckled. "Aye, just a few..."

Wiki fell into an empty chair. He hadn't completely fainted but it kind of looked like he'd logged off from life for a minute. His circuits were blown.

"I spent my youth far away from here. Very far away," Gale said softly. "I learned so much from so many amazing, peculiar teachers. One day I realized that I needed to give other children that unique opportunity. I needed to create a school with that kind of diverse, worldly faculty. Nobody is more passionate than our teachers. And wait until you get to the high school."

Now my mind was blown. My crackpot theory was right! But how many other teachers were there? And were any of them legendary heroes? Would Principal Gale ever tell us, or would we have to keep guessing? The image of that locked bookshelf in the library came into my mind. There were a lot of books in there. A lot. I started feeling light-headed. Don't faint, Javi. Don't faint.

Only Brady kept it together. "So that's why you have the Any Three People assignment every year. You're trying to find Andy so that you can summon more teachers."

Gale nodded. "Finding Brocéliandus is a safety issue first and foremost. But, yes, once we find Brocéliandus and his Chosen Ones, we ask that they help us summon a new teacher or two. But we can speak about that at another time."

"Cool, cool, cool. So what do we do about the pirate and the monster?" Brady asked, punching one fist into the other hand.

Principal Gale stood up and looked out the window at the wreckage. "Jekyll will be fine. We have been treating his condition for a long time, and, in all of his years here, this is his first flare-up. We will make sure it doesn't happen again, now that we know the one unlikely trigger." She looked over at the three of us. "I apologize about the pirate. He had us all fooled. But I spoke with him, and you three have nothing to fear. If he attempts to fool us again in any way, we will send him back."

"That pathetic sea robber," Scrimshaw muttered darkly. "Once a pirate, always a pirate, I say. And he has the nerve to call himself a captain! We should've sent him packing on day one."

"Why not just send him back now?" Brady asked. "Wait, is Blackbeard secretly the best groundskeeper of all time?"

Principal Gale chuckled. "Not exactly. Some of the teachers here were accidentally summoned like Mr. Teach, and each one gets the chance to stay on as faculty. Mr. Teach gets one more chance, because the temptation to use Brocéliandus's magic is powerful. I know it firsthand." She smiled at Ms. Kahlo and Mr. Scrimshaw, who looked dubious. "I can't blame any visitor for wanting to use it. But only you three can use it. And now he has been warned."

We were all quiet for a minute, taking in everything that had been said. And the fact that our school was weirder than we'd ever imagined. And that a monster from a book had just ripped a hole in my science classroom's wall.

Suddenly the silence was broken by Principal Gale's ringing phone. It was so jarring that all of us jumped a little bit in our seats. She picked up the phone, stood up, and started pacing as she spoke.

"Mm-hmm. Yes that sounds good. Okay." She paced and paced, and as she talked, she took the bell from the desk and placed it gently in the covered cage behind her desk. When she closed the cage it made a heavy locking sound. Fingers crossed that the cage was pirate-proof.

I let everything she'd just said sink in, and then, all of a sudden, a plan came together in my head. Not just a casual, why-don't-we-try-this plan, but an urgent, we-must-drop-everything-and-do-this-or-die plan.

She hung up the phone and looked at us. "Apologies. It sounds like I am needed in the cafeteria. I think we're clear though, yes? Please don't hesitate to come see me if absolutely anything suspicious happens. I'll be checking in with you regularly until this matter is resolved."

We nodded, said our goodbyes, and left the room.

"Okay, amigos," I said. "I hope you slept a lot last night. Because we have a long night ahead of us."

26

"I think I hear crickets outside."

"Okay, that means it's late enough."

"Let's go."

We were hiding in a big pile of costumes backstage at the high school theater. It was nighttime. And we were about to do something really, really stupid. I guess desperate times call for really, really stupid ideas.

"Okay, follow me," I said. I peeked out at the auditorium from behind the curtain. "The coast is clear. Vamos." We climbed off the stage and tiptoed through the dark auditorium toward the dim light coming from behind the doors ahead.

We'd spent hours waiting and waiting for the school

to empty. For most of that time we'd talked about Principal Gale's big revelation and tried to figure out other teachers who might be Andy-summoned visitors. So far we hadn't landed on any more (though I was still suspicious of Ms. Vlad), because they all probably used aliases. Then we tried to figure out which ones were weird enough to be from history or fiction, and they pretty much all were, so that wasn't helpful. Then we guessed which ones were accidents. (Ms. Vlad was definitely not the best English teacher of all time.) When we'd gone through every teacher we could think of, Wiki ran through all the reasons this was a bad plan and that I should let him be the plans guy. I could only put up with that for a few minutes, so we set off, probably to our deaths.

"This is really freaking me out," Brady whispered behind us. "I feel like Hyde is going to pop out of the shadows any second."

"Don't freak us out too," I loud-whispered.

"Yes, let's focus on the task at hand," Wiki agreed.

I creaked the center auditorium door open a bit, looked around, and then motioned for them to follow.

We were in the castle again. It was really cold and dank at night, and one thousand times spookier. It wasn't Hyde or Blackbeard that I was freaked out about—it was the rumors of all the mythical beasts kept in the basement. Had Principal Gale actually summoned some? I kept picturing a dragon crashing its head through a door and spitting fire at us. I wasn't exactly in the mood to become a dragon's midnight snack.

We made our way through the dark stone hallways, up a flight of stairs, and into the high school library. I could stomach medium-scary horror movies and slightly scary video games, but walking into an almost-pitch-black medieval library at midnight was a bit much for me. "It beats being butchered by Beardo," I kept repeating to myself, though it wasn't a very helpful mantra. Wiki was too busy analyzing everything to be scared, and Brady eats fear for breakfast, so I tried to borrow their bravery.

I traced my path back to the impossibly high bookshelf, and once I thought we were close, I pointed up. Brady shined her pocket flashlight into the darkness above. A glint! She tossed me a gym rope and we tied it between us like mountain climbers. Then we began our ascent into what felt like an infinite black hole. I didn't even bother counting shelves this time, focusing one hundred percent on gripping each one for dear life. If I fell I knew Brady would pull me up with the rope, but if she fell we were both done for. Shelf after shelf after shelf—it felt like we were climbing for hours. Finally we got to the top and rolled onto it panting like we'd just scaled Everest. Then Brady got to work while I caught my breath.

"Um, Javi," Brady said, as she dangled her arms over the ledge to open the shelf. "This bookcase is locked."

WHAT?! I almost jumped up screaming, until I remembered where I was. Did Mr. Bottom climb all the way up here and lock it? Was he Spider-Man? We took turns trying to open the bookcase in every way we could, but the lock was solid and the glass was extra thick. The longer we were up there, the more vertigo I was getting. I guess vertigo gets worse when you feel completely hopeless. "Well, there goes my plan. We're toast. I failed us."

"Not yet." I heard Brady fumbling around in her pockets, and then a beam of light shot out from where she was perched. Her pocket flashlight! "I'll read you the titles and you write them down." I would've hugged her if she wasn't my sister. "Okay, hold on to the opposite side of the bookshelf so you'll catch me if I fall." I took a step back to the other side and held on tightly. For a split second my brain reminded me that this could be the dumbest thing I'd ever done in my life. Muchas gracias, brain.

"Bad news," she said. "A lot of these books are so old that they don't have titles on the spine. Okay, here's one. Just a sec, it's hard to read it with the light reflecting off the glass. *Moby Duck?* I think one is *Moby Duck.*" I didn't have a pen, but I wasn't about to forget that title. What famous book is about a duck named Moby? "Here's another one. *Don Quickie?* Yeah, it says *Don Quickie.*" Do all famous books have dumb titles? "There are a bunch in other languages. And some are mostly faded out." She spent a few minutes silently searching. "Oh, here's one last one. *Molly Cat.*" Yes. All famous books have dumb titles.

The way down was a hundred times scarier than the way up, especially with the rope tied around my waist to remind me that falling could equal death. We made our slow way down, and it felt like it took years. Finally my feet touched ground, I let out a monster exhale, and Wiki asked, "Where are the books?"

"It was locked," Brady said, shaking her head. "But Javi wrote down the titles of the ones we could make out through the glass. Javi?"

"There were only three. *Moby Duck, Don Quickie,* and *Molly Cat.* Any of those have epic heroes in them? Maybe someone with laser eyes or super strength?" We started walking back toward the tables while Wiki mulled it over.

"Well, the first one is *Moby Dick*, not *Duck*." Bummer. I was hoping for a huge talking duck. "Moby Dick is a white whale, so I'm not sure why that book's up there, unless there's secretly an enormous leviathan living in an ocean under our school."

"There are only whales in that book?" Brady asked. "Are there talking fish too? Sounds more like a cartoon."

"No, the story's told by this sailor named Ishmael, and then there's Captain Ahab. He's this old, grizzled ship captain with a peg leg and a big scar running down his face. He's completely obsessed with whales and getting revenge on Moby Dick, the white whale who ate his leg."

"*Wiki.*" I gasped so long that I must have sucked up all the air in the library. "Fake leg. Giant scar. Whale obsession. Think about it."

It was like I cast a freeze spell on Wiki. He stood perfectly still except for his eyes, which raced back and forth as they got wider and wider and wider. "No. It can't be. That's ridiculous. Except. Except there's no other explanation. Mr. Scrimshaw? Our science teacher is Captain Ahab?"

"That's why he hates Blackbeard so much!" I said. "The dude has tussled with pirates before."

"Well, can he take on Barfbeard?" Brady asked.

Once Wiki got over the shock, he muttered, "I don't think so. He's definitely no hero, and unless Blackbeard turns into a massive whale, I'm not sure he could face off against him."

Then we heard whistling. Sometimes whistling is sunny and carefree and it mellows you out and brings a smile to your face. But if you hear whistling in an ancient castle's library late at night when it's perfectly dark, it's eerie and bloodcurdling and brings a look of complete and utter terror to your face. Brady slapped her hands over both of our mouths immediately and gave us a "don't move" look.

Who hung out in this nightmare library at night? It had to be a ghost. What else but a ghost? Maybe some old student had a dictionary fall on his head and died and haunted this place. "Que paraíso, esta biblioteca…" Except the ghost spoke Spanish and sounded like an old man. Weird ghost. Wait, I knew that voice.

"Señor Aleph," Brady whispered as quietly as she could. The head of Finistere's libraries. He was completely blind but could find any book in all three school libraries guided just by his memory. He was obsessed with books like no one I'd ever met, and honestly it didn't seem that weird that he was taking a stroll through the stacks this late at night. "If we stand perfectly still, he won't know we're here."

"¿Hay alguien ahi?" he asked from just a few feet away.

Chill, Javi. He can't see you. Calm down. Don't move. Not a muscle. Not. One. Muscle. Nope. Not happening. "Run!" I yelled, and the three of us made a mad dash through the stacks, past the tables, and out the door. Once we were on the other side I listened but heard nothing. He wasn't following us. Brady shoved me a little and shook her head. Yeah, not my best moment. "Okay, so Mr. Scrimshaw's not going to save us. What about Don Quickie, Wiki? Don Quickie and Molly Cat?"

Wiki pursed his lips. "You must have misread those titles. I don't recognize them. But even if I did, the chance that they would have epic heroes in them is almost nil. Think about it. Why would Principal Gale summon a knight or a brawny hero to teach us? Better a famous scientist or mathematician."

Yikes, Wiki was right. "Okay, but it was a good plan in theory," I protested. "It was—"

Footsteps. Not very far away. The sound of a door creaking open. Then shut. Then silence. Was Finistere a nightclub after midnight? Why did everyone wander around here at all hours of the night? At first I was spooked that we'd get caught. But then Brady pointed out the real issue.

"That was Principal Gale's door. If the noise came from over there, it had to be."

"There's only one person who would be sneaking into her office after hours," Wiki said.

Brady immediately started sprinting toward Gale's office, turning around and motioning to us when she realized we weren't following. Corner the scariest pirate ever in the dead of night? Not my idea of a good time. Then again, what choice did we have? It was either that or let him have the bell and eventually get murdered by mateys. And if there was one death I wasn't down with, it was murder by mateys. After groaning loudly, we joined Brady's race through the halls.

We heard another noise on our way over. It must have been the door shutting, because when we peeked around the corner to Principal Gale's hallway, a shadow was disappearing down the other end of the hall.

"We're too late," Wiki said, deflated.

"Only one way to find out," I said. Once we were sure the shadow was gone, we made our way to the scene of the crime.

27

"Are we sure this is a good idea?" Wiki asked. Standing in front of the principal's office and getting ready to break in, I had to admit, it was a valid question.

"Wiki!" Brady hissed. "We have to know if Blackbeard took the bell. We're doing the principal a favor." She pushed the door and it swung open. No lock? That wasn't a good sign.

I walked in first. It was pitch black, so I borrowed Brady's flashlight and we crept over to the cage where the bell had been hidden. The principal's office was absolutely terrifying in the dark. All of the things that made it awesome in the daytime made it a nightmare now. The shadows that the weapons and strange instruments cast made me want to tear out of there at full speed.

"Point the flashlight at the cage," Wiki whispered. I stopped staring at the medieval crossbow and having a panic attack and shined the flashlight on the cage.

"Whew. It's still here." We all let out a huge sigh of relief. "Now how secure is it?" Brady asked, examining every surface of the little prison. "He's going to come back for it at some point."

The cage was pretty interesting. It looked kind of like an ancient birdcage, except the bars seemed strong enough to hold a bear. It was so heavy that none of us could lift it even a centimeter off the ground. After studying it for a few seconds, we found a little door, which was almost invisible except for the small keyhole at its corner.

"It looks impenetrable. He would need to find the key," Wiki whispered. "Clearly it's with Principal Gale. She likely wears the key around her neck. Or puts it in a safe in the school basement. Or—"

"You mean this key?" It was the only thing in the principal's top desk drawer. I motioned to where I found it, and Wiki looked dubious. Brady grabbed it and ducked down to try it on the cage.

"There's no way the principal keeps the cage's key right next to the cage. This is her ultimate safe. Like I said, she probably wears it on her neck in a box that requires another key to open it, and—"

CLICK. "Yep, it worked," Brady said.

Wiki slapped his forehead. "My respect for the principal just dropped two notches. And here you trusted her to keep us safe?"

"Why would she make it so easy?" Brady asked. Opening the tiny door was difficult at first because it was heavy, and the bars scraped against each other as Brady tried forcing it. But then the door gave way and swung right open.

And as it opened, the cage laughed at us.

It wasn't exactly a human laugh. It made this noise when it creaked open like it was snickering at us. It was strange enough that we all jumped back.

"Did that cage just laugh at us?" I asked, spooked out of my mind.

"No, it...it sounded like it was calling a pet," Brady

said quietly. "Like, 'Here Fluffers. Tsk-tsk-tsk. Come here.'"

"Maybe this wasn't the best idea," Wiki whispered, scowling at us.

Then we heard a noise we'd never heard before.

It was the sound of wings, but they sounded different than bird wings. They sounded bigger. And more menacing. And there were a lot of them.

At first the sound was faint and off in the distance, but it was getting closer. And closer. The three of us completely froze, listening to it get louder and louder. Whatever it was, it was heading for us.

Wiki whispered, "Is it coming from the hallway or outside?"

Brady whispered, "I think it's coming from—"

And then, with a crash and a howl, a hideous flock of dark, winged beasts shattered the window, screeching as they came for us.

"RUN!" I yelled as we tripped over each other and then broke into a mad dash out of the room, racing through the stone hallway. I looked back and couldn't believe my eyes. There must have been fifteen of these furry, winged creatures chasing us, hissing at us, gaining on us. The sound of their flapping wings raised the hairs on my neck.

"This way!" I shouted, racing down the stairs, hoping we would lose them. But they came screaming down the stairs after us, floating ever closer. "Follow me!"

We scrambled down another hallway, took a right, and sprinted down another.

"Are you taking us somewhere specific?" Wiki asked, losing his breath.

"I sure am."

I was getting close. Mr. Loxley's economics classroom... Señora De Burgos's creative writing classroom... Mr. Fenrir's drama classroom...almost there...

We rounded another corner and got to my destination: Mr. Hotep's high school science class, one of the few classrooms in the high school with a door on it. And I noticed earlier that it had been left open.

"In here!" I yelled, and we practically threw ourselves into the room, the beasts only a few feet behind us, as I slammed the door shut and locked it. The beasts kept ramming their wings against the little window in the door, glaring at us and screeching.

Finally Wiki stepped back from the window and exhaled loudly. "Well, they won't be able to pierce through that small window, given their size and apparent strength, so we should be safe in here."

"What are those things?!" Brady screamed. "Summoning Mozart for dinner is one thing, but flying monsters chasing us through school? What the heck is going on?"

We both turned to Wiki out of habit.

"Don't look at me. I'm as lost and confused as you are. My only guess is that these creatures were once summoned through Andy. He summoned Jekyll and Ahab—it's clear that he can summon just about anyone. Or anything."

"Do you think Principal Gale summoned them?" Brady asked.

"She may have. Who knows what other creatures are lurking in the school."

"Hey, there's a gang of flying monsters right outside this door that want us in their bellies. There's no need to freak us out even more," I said shivering. "Now what do we do?"

"Nothing," Wiki said quickly. "We can only wait. If no one's ever seen them before, logic dictates that they'll have to leave before the school opens. So if they don't break through the door and kill us, hopefully they'll be gone by then. Since there is no other exit to this room, I think that's our only choice."

The creatures screeched again, as if they understood Wiki and didn't like his plan.

"It's going to be a long night," I said, sitting down on a table and realizing how exhausted I was. "A long, terrifying, screech-filled night. At least we got the bell before Blackbeard stole it."

"I didn't grab it..." Wiki said slowly. We both looked at Brady.

"We were about to get eaten by flying monsters! Of course I didn't have time to get it!" Brady screeched.

"So the bell is sitting in an open cage just waiting for Blackbeard to take it," Wiki groaned.

"Fiddlesticks," I said, burying my face in my arms and trying to sleep through the shrieks.

28

"This is definitely not a dream. But the flying monsters. That was a dream?" I was practically sleepwalking to school with Wiki, the two of us with massive bags under our eyes, stumbling groggily and trying not to fall asleep on the spot.

"No. No, that wasn't a dream either," Wiki said yawning. "I wish it had been, but we were definitely fully awake all night. They were all too real."

"I can't get their shrieking out of my head," I moaned. "I thought it would never end. I swear I still hear it now. Ugh, I wish the sandman would just punch me in the face with sleep."

We'd been stuck in the science classroom until

5:00 a.m., when the sun started peeking out and the flying furries finally flew away. We made 100 percent sure the coast was clear, then snuck past Gale's office, raced home, changed, told Dad our (fake) sleepover with Wiki was fun, and started walking back to school.

I guess this is what it feels like to pull an all-nighter when you're in high school. Except I bet studying for a test is a teensy bit less stressful than fending off monsters for hours and hours.

"Hey," Brady said breathlessly, catching up with us. She said she'd forgotten something in her room, ran home, and then ran back. I have no idea how she was so infuriatingly awake. She studied Wiki for a second and shook her head. "Stop looking so hopeless, Wiki— there's a pretty good chance we're in the clear."

"Oh?" Wiki asked, stopping and looking at her directly. "How did you come to that conclusion?"

"Well, I doubt that Blackbeard went back for the bell after hearing all the screaming, and when we tried sneaking into Gale's office this morning she was already in there. You know the minute she walked into her office she closed that cage, and there's no way Blackbeard's going to break into it. Good luck with the flying creepies, Mr. Teach."

Wiki looked unconvinced. "That cage was open for at least eight hours last night, and Blackbeard is desperate for that bell. For all we know, he was just waiting for someone else to trigger the monsters."

"I don't know, Wiki. I think Brady might be right," I said. "I thought we were dead meat until we tried to open that cage last night. Wow. I think I'm actually feeling kind of optimistic now."

Suddenly I felt wired. We might survive! I tried to do a cartwheel, but I just did a sloppy half-forward roll and then plopped on my stomach and started falling asleep.

"Come on, Javi," Brady said, kicking me lightly. "If we don't get to sleep, neither do you."

First period was awful. It was creative writing class with Ms. Sherry-Zadi, who usually taught for five minutes and then slipped into telling us a long, involved story for the rest of class. The stories were usually pretty awesome, but I was way too tired to listen to anything, so my face kept falling on my desk. I think she was kind of insulted when she realized I couldn't stay awake.

Second period was even worse. It was Ms. Vlad, so I couldn't show any weakness—now I was even more convinced she was an actual garlic-hating, fangs-for-days, neck-chomping vampire. And who knows, maybe if someone fell asleep in her class she would bite them and turn them into a mini Dracula. I had to somehow sit with perfect posture and with my eyes wide open, even though my entire body was screaming *Go to sleep, Javi!* as loud as it could. The only line that ran through my head the entire period was, "Must...stay...awake..." If we escaped Blackbeard's wrath, I wasn't about to get killed by Ms. Vlad. I doodled drawings of pirates getting summoned by Andy to keep myself awake. Why us, Andy? Why did you curse us with your friendship? And why couldn't you have been a magical hoverboard or a radioactive spider?

The three of us met at our lockers and headed to lunch. Wiki was this kooky mix of exhaustion and paranoia, like Blackbeard could jump out of any corner and murder us, but Wiki was almost too tired to care. Brady was full-on wired, skipping through the hall, humming a little song.

Then we saw Blackbeard at the end of the hall. He wasn't his usual wicked self—in fact, the guy was smiling innocently. Uh-oh. That's the last expression he should have had on his face today. Both Brady and Wiki noticed it too. Brady stopped humming immediately. Wiki's mouth opened a little and he shook his head slowly.

"Come on, we've gotta get to the bottom of this," I said. "Let's tail him."

We walked quickly until we were about ten feet behind Blackbeard, hiding behind some older kids who were walking right in front of us. That's when he started whistling to himself. It must have been some old pirate song, but it sounded extra annoying. Why was he whistling now, of all times?

Brady grabbed both Wiki and me by the collar and brought us in close. "Do you hear that?" she whispered.

"I know—it must be some pirate anthem," I whispered back. "It kind of sounds like Skidamarink-a-Doo."

"No, not that. That jingling sound. It's really light. Listen."

We tried to keep up while walking on our tiptoes. I strained to hear anything. Oh wait. Yeah. Yeah, that was definitely a jingle. That was definitely—

"The bell!" Brady whispered.

"No. Please no. NO," I wailed, as I felt my heart drop and flop around on the floor.

"That could be anything," Wiki said. "There are so many things that jingle." But his eye was twitching.

"Only one way to find out," Brady said.

She walked right up to Blackbeard and pushed him as hard as she could.

"Argh!" Blackbeard cried as he stumbled and fell, hard. I heard the jingling of what must have been the bell. His face turned dark and he muttered to himself, "Who dares cross the scourge of the seven—"

And then he saw it was us, and his face went smiley and sweet.

"Ah, good morning, you cute little ragamuffins."

"The bell, Blackbeard. I hear it in your coat," Brady said, pointing at him with a big scowl on her face.

"A bell? No, I'm sorry, I don't know what you're talking about. You must have heard my keys jingle.

Groundskeepers have a lot of keys to carry around." He stood up again, brushed himself off, and smiled. "Now, I hope you'll allow me to apologize for all of my past behavior. I'm a new man. I want to be a helpful member of our community."

Who was this guy?

Brady didn't look amused at all. Instead she quickly darted her hand out and shook his coat. The bell (or something that sounded exactly like it) rang more loudly.

"Once again," Blackbeard said too sweetly, "those are my keys. I appreciate you coming over to say hello though. Have a wonderful day." He bowed and walked quickly down the hall.

"He has the bell?!" I yelled.

"He definitely has the bell," Wiki said rubbing his forehead.

"We've gotta go straight to Principal Gale," I said, and started walking toward the high school. Wiki followed me.

"I left something at home," Brady said quickly. "I'll meet you guys there." She took off.

That was weird. We weren't allowed to go home at lunch—and she probably wouldn't make it back in time.

But I had no time to think about it. We had to solve the Mystery of the Smiling Pirate. To the principal!

29

"Well, you two had quite the night," Principal Gale said, sitting down at her desk. "I hope my pets didn't scare you too much." She smiled kindly.

She knew about our attempted robbery. Whoops.

"You call those pets?" I said. "They were going to kill us!"

She laughed. "They're actually completely harmless, but they're meant to frighten people away, so it looks like they did their job."

"What were those things?" I asked.

"Perhaps you should be starting with an apology instead," said a voice behind us. Mr. Scrimshaw—er, Captain Ahab—was standing next to her door. I yelped, then I nodded hello. He nodded back, looking super serious.

"No, there's no need for that," Principal Gale said, shooing the air. "To be fair, I now realize I should have explained why there's no need to worry. No one takes anything I place in here," she said, tapping on the cage behind her.

Wiki let out a quiet gasp and I saw why. The fabric was draped over the cage but peeking out of the corner was a familiar glint. The bell! It was still in the cage!

"We thought Blackbeard might have stolen it and—"

"He knows he cannot." Gale smiled at us again. "Rest easy. You made it through the hard part. If he tries anything else, he will be gone. And believe me, Blackbeard wants to stay."

"Breathe easy, lads," Ahab said, escorting us out of Gale's office. "If that pirate even looks at you the wrong way, he's got my harpoon to deal with. And I've used it on stranger foes than whales."

I felt like I was walking on air. "It's over. I can't believe it's over."

Wiki wasn't quite as excited as I was. "It's not over

until Blackbeard's returned to his home. Then I'll breathe easy."

I ignored him. I wasn't going to waste another day freaking out about it. I was exhausted enough as it was.

Bio was weirder than ever now that I knew who Mr. Scrimshaw really was. All of his extra-credit assignments made perfect sense now—he was still hunting Moby Dick as a middle school teacher! In class, Reba found footage of a very pale whale and it made Ahab so happy that all we did for the rest of the class was sing sea chanteys as he danced on his table, keeping the rhythm by stomping his fake leg. I didn't want to tell him, but I was almost positive Reba was showing him clips from a movie. At least Ahab was so excited he didn't notice me napping on my desk.

I spent lunch snoring with my face in my food, but even with the back-to-back naps, I was dead to the world by the time recess rolled around. Wiki was the same. We sat on the edge of the playground and tried not to fall asleep.

"Hey J-Train," Buddy Grimes said, looming over me. "I think your sister sprained her ankle. She asked me to come get you." He pointed toward the field on the other side of the school. Wiki and I jumped up and followed Buddy.

"How'd she sprain her ankle?" Wiki asked politely.

"I don't know, dude, I just heard her screaming for her bro. Now come on!"

Grimes was huge, but he was a pretty fast runner, and we had trouble keeping up with him. He took us past the recess yard and around the corner. I didn't see Brady but he pointed to the big shed in the back corner of the huge yard. "She's over there."

When we finally got close I had to slow down and catch my breath. "Wait! Wait...for me." I shuffled slowly toward the shed.

"Hold on. Why are we following Grimes?" Wiki whispered, between wheezes. "He's never once been helpful to anyone."

"Guys! Stop!" a familiar voice shouted. Rounding the corner of the yard was none other than Brady.

"Blackbeard has the bell!" she yelled. Wiki panicked, but I shook my head.

"Don't worry, we saw the—*mhmnnn mmfmnfm!*"

Something got thrown over my head. Someone grabbed my arms and put them behind my back.

Then I got thrown over someone's shoulder, and it all went dark.

30

"Almost...got it... Almost... There we go!" I yelled. I'd been trying to wrestle the sack off my head for who knows how long. It isn't easy when you're completely tied up!

I looked around. We were in a dark shed, and it smelled awful. Not just like dirt and manure though. Oddly, it smelled like slime from the sea. Wait... Sea stench... Blackbeard!

Brady was rolling around next to me, trying to jiggle the bag off her head as she groaned. The two of us had our arms and legs tied up in some pretty tight ropes. Where was Wiki?

"Brady! Let me try to help you!" I wriggled closer but

I couldn't do much. I wriggled until my feet were next to Brady's head, then I pulled the sack off after accidentally kicking her in the face a few times. She didn't care.

"Blackbeard! When I get my hands on him..." She growled.

"What happened?" I asked as I tried to shimmy my hands out of the ropes.

"It was a setup! Grimes was in on it. He lured you to the shed, and then when I got there Blackbeard snuck up behind you and pulled you into it. Then Grimes got Wiki. I almost got away, but that pirate runs crazy fast. Anyways, we're in deep doo-doo, because Blackbeard's probably heading to our house right now."

"But I saw the bell in Principal Gale's office. He can't do anything without it."

"It must have been a fake. Blackbeard's definitely got the real bell."

"How do you know?"

Brady paused for a second. "I...I just know. Trust me." She looked around the shed. "Wait. Where's Wiki?"

"I was about to ask you the same question."

Brady gasped. "Blackbeard's got Wiki. And the bell."

"Wiki? He's as good as dead!"

"We've got to break out of these ropes."

"Good luck with that," I said, hyperventilating a little. "I'm sure the most famous pirate of all time is pretty good at tying people up."

"Yeah, but you know what he's not good at? Putting us somewhere we can't break out of. Look around, Javi. We are literally surrounded by sharp things."

Little sis was right. There were hedge clippers and tree trimmers and even a machete. There were also dozens of puppy posters and plushies lining the walls. Wait, why was this entire shed full of puppy stuff? Was the most fearsome pirate of all time legitimately obsessed with puppies?

"There's our best bet," Brady said, motioning to the machete propped up against the wall. "Stop staring at the puppies and help me wriggle toward it."

Helping her was supremely awkward because all I could do was roll around on the floor of the shed. I felt like a rolling pin, going back and forth. I looked like an idiot. "Ugh, you're useless. I'll do it myself." Brady groaned. She hopped over to the machete—which is

pretty tough when your arms and legs are tied up—
and started pushing her back against it, trying to cut
her ropes.

"Hmmm, that always seems to work in the movies,"
I said.

"I thought so too. But I don't think I'm doing anything
really. This is dumb," she said. I started rolling on the
floor again. "But that's even dumber. Why do you keep
doing that?"

I didn't really have a good answer for her until I
noticed a pair of lawn scissors in the corner of the
shed. I squirmed over, pushed my back up against the
scissors, and eventually got them into my right hand.
Then I spent a while trying to get the angle right...
and...

"Ta-da!" I said, breaking free from the ropes.

"Wow, not bad, bro! You never save the day!"

"Thanks?" I said as I cut the ropes holding my legs
together and then snip-snip-snipped Brady's ropes
until she was free too.

"Vamonos!" Brady yelled, tearing out of the shed at
full speed. "Operation: Save Wiki!" I jumped up and

followed her. Wow, we'd been in there for a while—it was well past the end of the school day.

"We should tell Principal Gale!" I yelled breathlessly.

"We will once we stop Blackbeard and save Wiki!" Brady yelled back.

"Wait—we're going to try and stop Blackbeard ourselves?" Even though we were all running as fast as we could, a massive gulp formed in my throat.

The sun had almost set by the time we turned the corner to see our house. First I noticed that our front door was open. Then I noticed that Dad was outside planting some bushes. Then I noticed Dad was whistling a sea chantey.

Blackbeard.

"Dad! Why's the door open?!" I yelled, as I ran up to him.

"Hey kids!" he said. "How about a 'Hello, how are you, Dad'? Or a 'Hey Dad, you sure look thirsty, I'll go fix you a piña colada'? Why all the intensity? You're like cockroaches in a chicken dance."

Brady barely even looked at Dad. She just ran straight into the house. Dad looked confused.

"Wiki just stopped by with your super nice groundskeeper, Mr. Teach. He said you guys were helping him build a puppy petting zoo, but the blueprints were in your room. They're probably still up there right now looking for them. Teach is a big fan of yours, by the way. Says you're a great kid. Heck of a beard on that guy. Maybe I should stop shaving for five years and attempt one myself..."

"Dad! Did you just let an evil pirate run into the house?!" I asked. I was breathing heavily and my eyes were twitching so much I probably looked like I'd escaped from Alcatraz.

"A what? Did you just say *pirate*?"

I nodded and sprinted into the house.

Wiki was draped over one of Andy's chairs, looking like he'd just survived a tornado. The rest of the chairs were scattered all over the dining room, most of them tipped over. Andy sounded like he was growling. And Brady was kneeling in front of Wiki, trying to get him to snap back into our reality.

"Wiki. Did Blackbeard just..." I couldn't even complete the sentence.

Even though he wasn't fully there yet, Wiki nodded slowly. He mumbled to himself, almost too quietly to hear: "I had to summon them. I had no choice. He would've killed us. I had to summon them all. Fifteen of them." His eyes drifted slowly to our faces. "You just missed them."

I raced into our backyard, clambered up the fence, and peeked over the edge. There in the distance, heading into the woods, were Blackbeard and fifteen pirates of every shape and size. I could still smell their stench from where I was standing. In a few seconds they had all disappeared into the forest.

"Yeah, they escaped. They're deep in the woods by now," I wheezed, back in the kitchen. Brady clenched her face and her fists.

"I had no choice. He would've killed us. I had no choice." Wiki was still in a daze, mumbling to himself.

Exhausted, reeling, and still out of breath, I collapsed to the ground. For a while we were silent, catching our breath, trying to make sense of the situation. After what seemed like forever, Wiki lifted his head, looked at us, and spoke. "Well, we lost."

We sat in silence for a full hour until Dad told us to clean up for dinner.

The meal started out awkward and only got worse. As soon as Wiki left, Dad started grilling us. He couldn't figure out why the two of us had acted so weird earlier and looked so glum now. Every time he asked, we came up with a lie, but we were too beat to think up good ones, so they were mostly pretty dumb and barely made sense.

"So let me get this straight. While I was talking to Mr. Teach, his dog named Pirate snuck inside. He's the one that made the mess in the dining room. You freaked out because I'd let Pirate into the house, but then when you ran inside, he hit Javi in the face and ran out the back door. Mr. Teach chased him out, which is why I never once saw this dog. Do I have all of that right?"

"That dog is some bully," I said. But hearing the whole lie all at once, I realized how stupid it sounded. Andy let out a sad purr. I guess it didn't even make sense to him.

"You do realize that everything has been completely over-the-top bizarro for the last couple of weeks, right? What's your mom going to think when she gets back? I mean, to top it all off, it smells like sewage and rotting fish in this house today. Don't you find that odd? Sewage. And rotting fish. Are you running a sushi restaurant in the sewers? You know what, don't even answer that. I'm scared you'll say yes."

A sushi-tostones fusion restaurant. File that idea for later, Javi.

"You guys are grounded. Until you give me an honest account of all the weirdness happening, you can't hang out with Wiki, and you can't leave the house, starting immediately."

"Daaaaad..." Brady moaned. I echoed her moan.

"Don't even start with that. Once you give me a good explanation, you're free. That's all I need. The truth."

"Okay," I said nervously, clearing my throat. "What if I told you that this is a magic table that summoned Blackbeard the pirate, and he's about to kill us unless we team up with our principal, a famous artist, and a fictional sea captain to stop him first?"

"Go to your room," he said, pointing up the stairs.

Well, it was worth a shot.

"Wiki was right," I said as we walked upstairs. "We

lost. We're just going to sit in our rooms grounded until we hear Blackbeard break in, run up these stairs, and slice our throats. Then he'll go take over the world. I can't believe I thought this was all over. Well, I guess now it's really all over. For everyone."

I realized that Brady was completely ignoring me, pulling her walkie-talkie out of her backpack and speaking into it.

"Wiki, we make our move at ten. Meet us at the top of the hill. I'll bring supplies."

"Aunt Nancy grounded me too," Wiki's voice crackled.

"No excuses, Wiki. Javi, be ready by 9:45."

I turned to look at Brady. "Wait, what?"

"We're going to spy on some pirates."

Downstairs, Andy was trembling.

31

There was a soft knock half an hour after lights-out. When I opened my bedroom door, Brady stood there in full camo gear with shoe polish spread all over her face, carrying a camo backpack.

"Are we going deer hunting?"

She rolled her eyes at me. "Could you please wear something with darker colors at least? Rubber-duckie pj's are honestly the worst choice you could have made. Ever."

I closed the door, rummaged through my drawers, and put on dark jeans and a black shirt.

"Better," she whispered as we crept down the stairs.

We opened the front door slooooooowly. It probably

took us five minutes to get it wide enough to squeeze through. Then we shut it just as slowly.

Despite being completely terrified of what we were about to do, I have to admit, it was a beautiful night. The air was cool but not too cool, the moon was full, and the stars had all joined the party too. We snuck silently across the yard and through the path to the top of the hill. Wiki was waiting for us at the top, looking pretty terrified himself. He was wearing his dad's oversize camouflage army jacket and dark pants. Brady hugged him.

"See? You get it. Javi doesn't get it. You get it." Wiki just froze. It was awkward.

"This is all my fault. All of it. Blackbeard. His crew. I had to summon them. I had no choice," he finally said.

"Wiki! Snap. Out. Of. It." Brady snapped her fingers over and over in front of his face. "These guilty vibes aren't helping one bit. Relax. We need your brain sharp if we're going to do this."

"I've been standing here contemplating how danger-ous and nearly impossible this mission is," Wiki whispered. "It's very dangerous. And nearly impossible."

Brady gave him the arched eyebrow. "Impossible? Sure, the forest is huge, but you're forgetting who we're dealing with here. These are pirates. They're loud. And feisty. They don't exactly hide in the shadows."

"Well, it's incredibly dangerous, at least," he shot back. "What has everyone always said to us growing up? What does every single adult say literally every time someone mentions the woods? 'Don't go into the woods at night.'"

"Aunt Nancy loves the woods," I said. "She never says anything about going to the woods at night. She'd probably high-five us right now."

"Okay, but everyone else in this town does," he muttered.

"Well, I'm no less freaked out than you are, but I don't think we have a choice," I said. "It's either find out the pirates' plan or wait for them to invade our house and destroy Andy."

Wiki put up his finger like he was about to say something, then instead just sighed, shook his head, and followed us down the hill and into the woods. "For the record, I did not endorse this idea," he muttered.

"Let's see. We saw them go into the forest...here," Brady said, pointing to an opening in the trees. She then pulled two flashlights out of her backpack and handed them to us, taking a third for herself.

"They'll spot us for sure if we're flashing these around," I whispered.

"We need to track them. We're not about to start running around the woods in the dark, hoping we don't trip on a pirate."

Wiki sighed. "You're both right. We'll have to proceed with only one flashlight turned on—follow their trail but minimize our visibility."

Since Brady brought the flashlights, she got to hold the one we used. It was fine by me—I didn't want to be in front drawing all the attention.

For a while, following the pirates' tracks was surprisingly easy—there was a clear path of broken branches and trampled leaves, and the faint stench of rum and sewage. Brady gave us a few "I told you it was going to be easy" looks as we made our way deeper and deeper into the woods. Then at some point we must have followed the wrong broken branch, because suddenly we found ourselves next to some huge, oddly menacing trees, completely lost without any trail to follow. We circled the scary trees a few times, making sure we hadn't missed a clue, and got down on our hands and knees, exploring all the branches and leaves on the ground. Nothing.

Wiki put his hand on his forehead as he shook his head. "Lost? Check. Spooky location? Check. Wanted dead by a group of bloodthirsty pirates? Check. Tonight is going incredibly well. Thank you for your amazing plan, Brady."

"This wouldn't have happened if we'd used three flashlights instead of one, genius!" Brady yelled, throwing her hands up in the air.

"Tell me you brought a compass in that bag full of stuff." Wiki sighed.

Brady made a face. "I've got a bunch of rope."

"Rope? We're not spelunking in caves."

"Papi always says, 'Never leave home without rope.'"

"I think it's 'Never leave home without keys,'" I whispered.

"Well, this was an enormous waste of time," Wiki huffed.

"Was it?" Brady asked, going from Ragey Brady to Jolly Brady instantly. I could see her smile reflecting the moonlight. "Shh!"

Sure enough, we started hearing pirate voices. We froze, then started walking very slowly toward them, trying our best not to trip or make noise. Eventually we could make out what the voices were saying. And we definitely recognized the loudest one.

"The key is sounding like a harbor seal with really bad indigestion, Bill," Blackbeard said. "Really burp it out."

"Yarrr harrr harr me hearties, avast!" a booming voice said.

"You're getting there!" Blackbeard said excitedly. "Now, let's all try that 'yar har har' again. Remember, it's extra spine-chilling if you say it like a bloodthirsty maniac."

"But we *are* bloodthirsty maniacs," a rough voice replied.

"Very true. But more of a loud, boisterous maniac. You might even want to cross your eyes and stick out your tongue a little bit as you say it. Think *rabid dog*. Ready, on three. One, two, three—"

"Yarr harr harrrrr!" erupted through the forest.

"Well, that gave me chills," Brady whispered.

"Shh," Wiki whispered back.

"Very good, mateys. Remember, we all call each other *matey*. And I think we pretty much call everyone else matey too. *Matey*'s an important word. If we had notebooks I'd ask you to write that one down and underline it."

"Pirate speak sounds a little idiotic, wouldn't you say?" a gruff voice said.

"Completely idiotic," Blackbeard agreed, "but people here won't believe that we're pirates unless we talk like that."

At this point we'd snuck behind a fallen tree that overlooked their camp and could make their faces out in the light of their campfire. Usually seeing faces lit by a campfire meant I was roasting marshmallows and singing hokey songs with friends, but these were the last fifteen people I'd ever invite over for s'mores. First off, multiply Blackbeard's sewer stench by fifteen. Then throw in a bunch of sour or just plain evil-looking faces with mucky beards and the worst breath. And then tack on nonstop belching and gross, gargly laughing. Thanks for ruining campfires forever, Beardo. Most of the pirates were sitting on stumps or on the ground in a semicircle around the fire, with Blackbeard standing at the front, wearing the wildest look in his eyes.

"So what's the plan, boss?" a small, snickering pirate asked.

"Well, apparently I need to buy a big hat and a parrot to put on my shoulder, and one or two of you will need peg legs—I'll explain that concept later."

"No, I mean the plan."

"Ah. Right, right, of course. Well, gather around, lads." He motioned to the pirates who'd been having their own conversations and they immediately ran to his side like he was a general in the army or something.

"As I told the lot of you before, that table whisked us all into the future more than three hundred years. And a lot has changed. It's far easier to be a pirate these days. For one, there's no competition. For another, we don't have to risk our lives boarding ships and looting privateers anymore. There are far easier ways of getting rich."

"Aye, but are they as fun?" asked Bill.

"Bill, if we do this right, we can buy a ship, buy our own private island, buy a thousand puppies, and then have fun, all day every day."

The pirates whistled and clapped.

"Here's the rub, mateys. We can rule the world here, and cause lots of mischief in the meantime, but first we have to make sure no one's sending us back, and we have to be free of our shackles."

"Who wants to send us back?"

"Someone who's about to get the Blackbeard treatment. And if you think pirate speak is wild, wait until I tell you guys about walking the plank." He laughed, sending chills up my spine.

"And what's this about shackles?" the tall pirate asked.

"The table," Blackbeard growled. "You don't realize it yet, but we're trapped in this town. None of us can wander freely while the table exists. We need to destroy it to be free."

"No!" Brady whispered loudly. "Not Andy!" She looked at us with tears forming in her eyes.

"Hey, Roger," one of the pirates closest to us

whispered. An especially large pirate turned to him. "Pass me some of the boy's grub, eh?" The big pirate handed him something that I couldn't quite make out in the darkness. "What'd the boss say this is called again? A sandwich?" The big pirate nodded. Sandwich? Did they raid my fridge before they left? Was that my award-winning sandwich in his grubby, disgusting hands? "When this is all over, how about we make the boy our chef and force him to make us sandwiches all day?"

"NEVER!" I screamed at the top of my lungs. Oops.

For a second everything seemed fine. Maybe the pirates thought it was one of them. Then they all went completely silent. I looked to my left, and Wiki was glaring at me like he wanted to squish my head.

"What was that?" the fat pirate asked.

"It appears we have visitors, gentlemen. Spies. Very, very amateur spies. Shall we show them what we do with spies?"

"*Aye!*" the pirates all chanted at the same time, raising their fists in the air.

"Bill, Roger, head toward the noise. The rest of you, spread out—I doubt this spy is alone."

As my eyes darted around frantically, trying to figure out how we'd get out of this mess, I noticed a shadow behind a tree across from us. The shadow from before.

"I'm not heading anywhere with this stinky heap," Bill seemed to say. "He smells almost as bad as his mother." The voice clearly came from the shadow behind the tree, but no one else seemed to notice.

Roger swung around to face Bill. "I bathe three times a month, ya blubbering buffoon! And leave my mum out of this!" He tackled Bill and the two began wrestling.

"Don't partner me up with Stupid Sam," the shadow said in another pirate's voice. "We'll get lost before we leave the camp."

"Stupid?" Sam said, looking over at the pirate next to him. "Is this because I can't tell my right from my left? That's it!" He head-butted the man and then they rolled around on the floor choking each other.

Soon all the pirates were either wrestling or trying to break up the fights.

"Vamonos!" Brady yelled. "Go, go, go!"

There's nothing like the threat of being dismembered by a bunch of pirates to get you running faster than you ever have in your entire life. The three of us vaulted out of our hiding place and shot through the forest like bullets. We had two advantages—we knew the forest better than them, and that talking shadow seemed to be on our side. They had one advantage—they were actual, real-life pirates. If I was a betting guy, I would not bet on the three of us.

At first it felt too easy—that shadow must have really done a number on the pirates, because at least thirty seconds passed between us jetting and Blackbeard screaming, "Enough, you imbeciles! Find them!"

Just as we were getting our hopes up that we'd escaped, a huge, sweaty pirate jumped in front of us, and in one move scooped up Brady with one arm, held her against his gross stomach, and put the sword to her throat.

"Don't move another inch or the girl gets it!" he said quietly. "Haven't you heard it isn't wise to anger a pirate, kiddos?"

Wiki shot back, "Pirate? You're not a pirate. You don't talk like a pirate."

The pirate suddenly got an awkward look on his face, almost embarrassed.

"Oh, uh, right. Ahem. Yarrr me heartos! Do as I be sayin' or she runs the plank! Then it's straight to, um, Daddy Jones's locker. Arr harrr! Now... OUCH!"

The distraction gave Brady enough time to gather her wits. She gave the pirate's arm a deep Brady-bite, then, when he dropped her, she stomped on his foot, hard. The pirate crumpled over, holding his arm and his foot awkwardly.

"Run!" Brady shouted and the three of us took off. There were no pirates in sight, and at last we could see the field beyond the forest. We sprinted the last bit until I tripped on a tree root, knocking the wind right out of me. When I picked myself up, Brady and Wiki were laughing and cheering as they leapt out of the forest and back into the meadow. "We did it! We did it!"

Then two more pirates came out of nowhere and grabbed them.

32

I stood frozen at the edge of the woods for a
long time, until it was quiet. I'd watched helplessly as
the pirates dragged my screaming friends back into the
forest, and I was too petrified to do a single thing about
it. And now Wiki and Brady were probably shish kebabs.

"What have I done?" I moaned.

"It's what you're about to do that's important, Javi."

I looked up, and there was Aunt Nancy standing
above me, holding out her hand and smiling.

"Aunt Nancy? Was that you before, with the pirates?
And where are they?"

"Let's focus on that second question first, hmm?
If you'll kindly follow me, I'll reunite you with our

friends. Just promise me you won't scream again." I nodded sheepishly and gave her my hand. She lifted me up, quickly brushed the dirt out of my hair, and nodded once.

I followed her through the woods, but she walked so fast I practically had to run to keep up. After a while, she stopped, put one finger to her mouth, and whispered, "Shhhhh." We crept quietly for a while, hearing the sound of voices get louder and louder. Finally we came to a row of trees with a clearing ahead.

"Wakey wakey, ya lily-livered hornswoggles," a familiar voice said. Wiki and Brady were tied to trees facing the pirates' camp. Blackbeard was standing over them looking especially ferocious.

"What say ya, boss—can we kill him now?" the tall pirate said, pointing at Wiki with his sword.

"No, that would be too boring. After everything these morons have put me through, they deserve a spectacular death. Well, this one and his friend do, as soon as we find him."

Awesome. A spectacular death. Can't. Wait.

"But for now, let's review our nefarious plan. I want

these two to hear all about the fear and suffering their teachers and friends are about to go through."

"I've never understood this section in stories, where the villain reveals his plan to the hero, who then escapes and knows just how to stop them." Wiki was awake and talking to himself. Blackbeard heard, though.

"Ha! 'Tis called 'hubris' or 'tragic pride.' It usually leads to the downfall of the villain," Blackbeard said. Wiki gave him a look of sheer surprise. "Ya don't suppose any pirates can read now, can ye? I've probably read thrice the books you have, ya pretentious pile of dog meat." He then got really close to Wiki's face. "The difference here is that your fate is sealed, boy. You're in the middle of the woods, tied up with Bill's famous Deadman's Knot, which no one has ever escaped from, surrounded by murderous pirates. Explain to me exactly how you're going to escape and save the day."

Wiki looked around and then hung his head in surrender.

"Sorry, lad, but this story doesn't end well for you."

"That's the last thing I'm gonna say to you before I defeat you." Uh-oh. Brady was awake.

"The spitfire awakens! Ah, but how I missed you. Gents, meet Brady, the future terror of the seas and Queen of Pirates. All hail, Queen Brady!"

"'Tis an honor, m'lady," said a couple of pirates as they genuflected.

For a second Brady was genuinely touched and might have even blushed a little. But then she went into Brady mode and spit in one of the pirate's faces. The pirate slowly wiped the spit off his cheek. I was sure Brady was about to get skewered and almost screamed. Instead he looked at her in awe. "You're the bravest kid I've ever met. All hail Queen Brady, indeed!"

Blackbeard motioned to the crew. "All right, me hearties, come gather round, and let's review the plan." The pirates gathered around the fire a dozen or so feet in front of us, and Blackbeard explained how they were going to hunt down the principal in Finistere's endless maze of hallways and make her walk the plank.

"We're gonna escort her all the way to the ocean? Are we gonna build a pirate ship too?"

"Argh, Teddy, why'd I even bother summoning you? You're deadweight. Anyone who's not a blathering idiot see where I'm going with this?"

"There's a plank somewhere in the school. And whatever 'walking the plank' means, that's how we get rid of that landlubber."

"Precisely, Bill! And bonus points for using pirate words." Bill nodded and winked.

"So what's the plan?"

Blackbeard pulled out a blueprint of our school that he must've stolen from the library. He'd already marked the whole thing up with arrows pointing to different places. He then whipped out a bunch of Monopoly tokens and set them up around the map. Each token represented a pirate. (Teddy spent five minutes arguing about how he should be the dog, not the thimble.) One by one, Blackbeard showed his crew where each one of them would be positioned and how they would all sneak through the school. I wasn't close enough to the map to see what he was talking about, and I bet Wiki and Brady weren't either.

"And remember—stay alert until we get to the field.

The forest witch is cunning and dangerous—but powerless outside the woods. Now, questions about the plan?"

"You mentioned something about the table earlier," a fat pirate said.

"Ah, yes. While most of us are at the school, One-Eyed Bob and Dagger Jack will be heading over to the pirate queen's house, get the table, and meet us at the rendezvous point. And once the principal walks the plank, we destroy the table once and for all."

"Never!" Brady yelled.

"Ah, don't fret, Queen of Pirates. We'll build you a new table just like it on our ship." Blackbeard laughed.

"Hey, boss. One last question," Bill said quietly. "Do we know destroying the table will free us? What if it just sends us all back instead?"

Blackbeard put a hand on Bill's shoulder. "Great question, Bill. I've wondered that too, and it's a risk we have to take. It's the price we have to pay for freedom. Right, boys?"

"Aye!" they chanted.

"Now, there's no time to lose. If we're lucky, maybe we

can find her before the children get to school. Rex and Baldy, stay here and tend to the kids. I'll have Bill come back and get you when it's time."

"The rest of you, swords in."

The pirates who had swords drew them and held them out over the campfire so that they all touched in the middle. The fire reflected on them, and despite being terrified, I had to admit that it looked really, really cool. All at once, the pirates chanted:

We are the scourge of the seven seas.
We are the terror of the West Indies.
We are the storm, the lightning, the thunder.
We're Blackbeard's men, let's tear the world asunder!

They all raised their swords and let loose a hideous scream.

"Onward, lads! And let's get back into character. We'll practice as we go. Bill, start us out!"

"Yarr, ye'll be walkin' the plank in no time, ya lily-livered fools!"

The pirates then started their march through the

forest to our school, saying dumb pirate catchphrases the whole way.

The two leftover pirates turned to Wiki and Brady.

"Those ropes tight enough for ya there?" Baldy asked. (He had to be Baldy. Dude had zero hair.) Brady growled at him. "Good."

Rex, a big pirate who looked oddly sweet, sat in front of them. "We'll be spending quite a while together, so I thought maybe you could answer me a few questions."

Wiki nodded awkwardly. "Um...sure?"

"Excellent. Now, for starters, Blackbeard mentioned something called the internet. What exactly is that?"

Wiki groaned. "Do you understand the basic concept of a computer?"

"Nope."

"How about electricity—did Blackbeard explain electricity yet?"

"Nope."

"Okay, but you understand what a basic machine is, right?"

"Machine?"

Wiki groaned even more loudly. "This is going to be a long night."

33

Ugh. I took a few steps back and punched a tree in frustration. Ow.

"Have a seat, Javi. There's no need to lose hope," Aunt Nancy said.

I sat down and looked at her. "Okay, let's review the situation. My best friend and my sister are tied up, and it's just a matter of time until they're skewered by pirates. It's all my fault because I couldn't keep my stupid mouth shut. And how am I helping? I'm talking to Wiki's aunt, who might be a forest witch with actual superpowers—so clearly I've lost my mind. Now am I allowed to lose hope?"

"Not yet," Aunt Nancy laughed.

"Okay, then let's not forget that it's me who has to save them. Not Wiki, the brains. Not Brady, the muscle. Javi, the stomach. The hungry dummy who just kind of hangs out with them and cooks tostones. Now I've definitely lost hope."

Aunt Nancy stood up and walked a slow circle around me, studying me like she was a lion. (Probably a nice, vegetarian one.)

"Now, I agree that Wiki's the brains and Brady's the brawn, but do you not realize your role in the trio? It might be the most important of all."

I scratched my head. "I guess I make a mean triple-decker peanut butter, banana, and sauerkraut sandwich. Is that important?"

Aunt Nancy laughed and shook her head. "Who solved the mystery of the school? Whose curiosity led to the truth about Finistere's teachers? And who came up with the plan to solve that mystery?"

I thought about it. "I guess I did?"

"Yes, you did. Because you are..." she looked at me expectantly.

"...a B+ chef!"

"...an artist, Javi. You're creative. Insightful. You like to make beautiful, delicious things, and you have a very different way of looking at the world. You're much smarter than you realize, it's just a different kind of intelligence than Wiki has. Personally, I think you're the one who actually woke up Andy. He's taken quite a liking to you."

"You don't know that. You haven't even met Andy."

Aunt Nancy stood up and patted the tree behind her. "Javi, I've known Brocéliandus for a very long time. A very, very long time. Remember when he purred at me that night I stopped by?"

"Oh yeah! I thought that was weird. So are you a wizard or something? Did you make Andy out of the tree? And why do you make that colossal crashing sound when you disappear into the forest?"

"Perhaps we should tell stories later. Your two friends are waiting for you to save them. And they trust that you can do it. As do I."

I looked back into the clearing. Baldy was sharpening his sword with a rock and glaring at them while Rex sat in front of Wiki, learning about the internet as he played with his sword.

"Can you help me?"

Aunt Nancy shook her head. "I'll leave it to you to save your friends. I have complete faith in you, Javi. Now, time for that mysterious crashing noise." She winked.

In the blink of an eye Aunt Nancy disappeared into the shadows and then there was that sound, like a tank trampling through the trees.

I turned back to the pirate camp, stood as tall and threateningly as I could, gathered up all my bravery, and walked right into the clearing.

Brady and Wiki looked over, and their jaws dropped at the exact same time. The pirates looked over, and Baldy got a huge smile on his face.

"That's the third one! Waltzed right into our camp. We'll be heroes!"

"*Stop*," I said in my loudest, most intimidating voice (which wasn't super intimidating, to be perfectly honest). "Untie my friends or you will suffer the wrath of Javi, the greatest wizard in the land."

Rex looked a little nervous, but Baldy just laughed.

"Great wizard, eh? Well, show us one of your magic tricks."

"You...uh, you don't want to see my magic—it's too dangerous." Uh-oh, I really should've thought this through before I decided to do a standoff. "If I snap my fingers, something...something super deadly will happen."

Rex looked afraid. Baldy laughed harder. "Oh yeah? Snap those fingers, boy. Snap 'em. I dare ya."

I raised my hand, fingers ready to snap. "You have until the count of three to run before I snap." I tried to look serious and threatening. I'm guessing I looked the opposite. "One..." Rex stood up just in case I was serious. Baldy crossed his arms against his chest and stood firm. "Two..." Rex started backing away slowly. Baldy just smiled wickedly and shook his head. "Two and a half..." Okay, what was I going to do now? What could I do but—"Three!" SNAP.

Rex and Baldy's eyes both went wide and Rex screamed, "Run!" Baldy fell on his butt, then scrambled to his feet and ran away at full speed, Rex following him.

"That's right! Run away! Ha!" Wow, I couldn't believe that worked!

I walked over to Brady and Wiki. Brady had a huge

smile on her face, but Wiki looked as terrified as the pirates.

"Wiki, it's me, Javi. I'm not really a great wizard all of a sudden. Chill out."

Then I noticed they were both looking behind me. When I turned around, three epic warriors were entering the pirate camp, glaring at the pirates. Well, two epic warriors and a kid. There was a guy dressed up like an ancient Asian warrior and wearing some seriously rad armor, an Egyptian queen who looked very familiar, and a boy in a white wig who was maybe a sidekick. Wait, not any boy...

"Kid Mozart! And you brought your superhero friends? Is this real life?" I checked my forehead to make sure I didn't have a fever.

Kid Mozart dashed over and gave me a hug. "Looks like we got here just in time. Now let's get our friends loose."

The ancient warrior did a flip and two somersaults, landed right in front of Wiki and Brady, and in one move pulled out a huge curved sword and sliced both trees. All of the rope fell into a pile.

"How in the world did you find your way back to our time?" Wiki said, rubbing his rope-burned arms.

"You think you're the only one with plans?" Brady said, strutting over with a huge smile. Kid Mozart gave her a hug.

"It was all Brady," he said. "She summoned us secretly so we could be reinforcements if things got dire."

"Remember when I pushed Blackbeard and then shook his coat this morning? I did that to ring the bell. That's why I raced back home 'sick.' I had summoned these three."

"So the bell worked even from far away. But what about the place cards?" I asked.

"I'd planted them right after you guys left for school. That's why I had to catch up with you."

I nodded my head in amazement. Wow, I had to hand it to her—it was a pretty genius plan.

Wiki looked happier than I'd ever seen him. He hugged Brady tightly and then realized what he was doing, took a step back, and coughed awkwardly. "Thank you, Brady. You—you saved the day." Then he looked around and tried to recover. "Glad to have you back, Kid Mozart. But who are your friends?"

Brady looked over at the man with ancient armor who was studying the blade of his sword, and the Egyptian queen who was surveying the scene.

"You don't recognize my personal hero? This is Cleopatra, queen of Egypt. One of the smartest, greatest rulers of all time. I thought she'd be good for our team." Cleopatra smiled and nodded at us.

"It is good to meet you. We have work to do, if we are to defeat the pirates," Cleopatra said. I waved awkwardly. Wiki's eyes couldn't have gone wider.

"And he's from the place card you wrote for the assignment, Wiki," Brady said, pointing at the armored guy. "You did a report on him earlier this year, and I remembered you yakking about him for weeks on the walk to school. I knew we needed someone to face pirates, so who better than a ninja?"

Wiki's face got super solemn and he knelt on one knee. Looking up at the warrior, he asked, "Hattori Hanzō, is that you?"

The warrior nodded once, as solemn as Wiki, then went back to studying his blade.

"Um, I'm blanking—who is this guy?" I asked. I guess

I usually just ignored Wiki when he was talking about school stuff.

"Hattori Hanzō," Wiki said in a soft voice, still obviously in awe. "Probably the greatest ninja of all time. We are honored, Mr. Hanzō."

He looked at each of us very seriously, and then quietly said, "There is no time to waste. What of the pirates?"

Brady's face went from family-BBQ-Brady to warrior-empress-Brady. "Gather around, everyone," she said, motioning for us to huddle. "Here's the situation. Blackbeard and his crew are hunting down Principal Gale and forcing her to walk the plank. Then they're going to try and destroy Andy. Our table. And then it's world domination time. But none of that's going to happen, because they messed with the wrong kids." She slammed her fist into her palm for emphasis. "Now, was your mission successful?"

"The table is hidden deep in the school," Hanzō said. "We have bought ourselves a little time. But perhaps only a little, if this pirate is as clever as you say he is." Brady had them hide the table? Wiki let out a low whistle, clearly impressed.

"Now we must strategize," Cleopatra said. "If my math is correct, we have two adults and three children against fifteen of the most dangerous pirates in history. I can hold my own, and Mr. Hanzō will make short work of some of them, but we need to even the odds."

"Reinforcements," I said. "We need to gather the teachers. At least, the ones we know that Andy summoned. Ahab would probably be pretty useful, and Frida Kahlo seems like she could kick some serious butt. And Ms. Vlad's definitely a vampire, so she could take on a few of them."

"Javi," Wiki groaned, "your vampire theory is almost as annoying as your sandwich theory. A whaling ship captain and a famous painter aren't going to be a ton of help against pirates. And Ms. Vlad is just a mean English teacher."

"*Don Quickie. Molly Cat*," I muttered to myself. "We need to solve that riddle to unlock those characters for the boss fight." Kid Mozart raised an eyebrow. Clearly the dude didn't play video games. "*Don Quickie.* That book sound familiar to any of you guys?" It was a shot in the dark, but why not?

"Don Quixote?" Kid Mozart asked, perking up. "The knight? My father used to read that book as we traveled to my concerts. It was his favorite."

"Don Quixote!" I said, jumping up. "The painting in Dad's room!" Brady high-fived me as we both realized it at the same time. There's this painting of a knight on a horse and his little sidekick on a mule that seems to be on the wall of every Puerto Rican house. Brady and I asked Dad about it once and he told us it was Don Quixote, the most famous hero in Spain, from one of the most famous books of all time. "A ninja, a warrior queen, and a legendary knight can take on those pirates—let's go find Don Quixote!"

"There is no time to lose, then," Cleopatra said. "You, Brady, and I can gather up the teachers. Hanzō, Kid Mozart, and Wiki will head straight to Blackbeard to ensure he doesn't murder the principal."

Wiki nodded. "Meet us at the pool."

The pool? All of us turned to Wiki. "Dude, this might not be the best time to perfect your backstroke," I said.

"Think about it. He wants to make the principal walk the plank. What's the closest thing a school has to a plank?" Right! Brady and I nodded excitedly but all of our guests still looked confused, so we had to explain what a diving board was, and then explain what a plank was, and then explain to Hanzō and Cleopatra exactly what pirates were. Once we were all caught up, we jumped out of our huddle.

"To the school! And the pirates! And probably our deaths!" I yelled, and we took off through the forest at full speed.

34

The action-movie music was blaring in my head. I looked around as we dodged trees and headed toward the morning light in the distance. An ancient queen sparkling with epic jewelry, a legendary warrior with katana swords sheathed in his epic armor, and a brilliant musician kid in a powdered wig—some hero squad we were! For all the headaches and nightmares Andy had caused us, he did score us some memorable new friends.

We practically exploded out of the woods and made a mad dash across the field toward Finistere. The sun was rising behind the castle and for a minute it felt like we were heading right into a fairy tale, not the exact opposite. The school grounds were quiet, and even though I didn't have my watch on, I'd bet it would be another hour or more until the students were here. Hopefully the teachers we needed came to work early. I didn't really peg Ahab for a morning person, but I imagined that whaling ship captains never had the luxury of sleeping in.

We parted ways at the middle school entrance. Wiki, Kid Mozart, and Hanzō snuck toward the high school, while Brady, Cleopatra, and I tried opening the middle school doors as quietly as we could. *Creeeeeeak.* "Not a good start," I whispered to myself. Cleopatra winced and nodded. We tiptoed into the school one after another. Brady didn't make a sound and was an A+ ninja, Cleopatra was stealthy except for her clanky jewelry, which made her a B+ ninja, but I would've been expelled from ninja school and never invited back. I walked as quietly as a full-sized T. rex doing the cha-cha, stumbling all over the place in my attempts to walk in silence. Halfway down the main hallway, Cleopatra motioned for us to stop.

"The pirates have never seen me before, so I can pretend that I work here. It's better if you sneak ahead a bit while I provide backup and guard the rear. If any pirates start to threaten you, I'll let them feel the wrath of Isis." I glanced at her steely eyes and instantly felt bad for any pirate who touched us.

The mood quickly shifted from our adrenaline-pumping race through forest and field to the quiet terror of being caught by a pirate in a classroom. I hoped Cleopatra had good eyes, because I bet a pirate could stab us a hundred times before she caught up with us.

"The closest teacher is Mr. Scrimshaw—um, Ahab. He's only two hallways away," I whispered to Brady as we turned the corner to another hallway. "Once we get him, Ms. Vlad and Ms. Kahlo are close by. Hopefully one of them knows where Don Quixote's classroom is, and we can head there last." Brady nodded and we started making our way down the hall, when two pirates came out of a door at the other end of it. Yikes! We ducked into an empty classroom and waited until they walked by.

"No sign of them here either, eh?" one said.

"We've got our crew spread across every floor in this school. We'll find her. And once we do, we'll see what this walking-the-plank business is all about."

"Blackbeard seems pretty keen on it, but I doubt it's as rewarding as a good old-fashioned cannonball to the buttocks."

"That's a good point right there," the other pirate said.

The school was officially crawling with pirates! After their voices got far enough away, we peeked out of the classroom and got into super-stealth mode, practically slithering down the halls. Every few steps we'd listen carefully for any noise or see if we caught a whiff of pirate stench. No other pirates seemed to be in the area, so after we got to Ahab's hallway we sprinted to his room and practically tumbled into it. Ahab was writing something on the chalkboard but whirled around when he saw us walk in. He immediately knew we were all in trouble.

"Blackbeard got the bell and he summoned his pirate friends and they captured us but a ninja and a legend saved us but they were too late because the crew already left for the school and now they're here and they probably have Principal Gale and they're trying to kill her plus destroy the table." I vomited the words out as I hyperventilated.

"Blackbeard!" Ahab yelled, crushing the chalk in his hand. "I told them a thousand times, never trust a pirate. Well, now we have some work to do."

Ahab marched over to the helm of his ship deck and grabbed his rugged captain's hat. Then he walked to the chalkboard and took down the giant harpoon that he had on display. Finally, he yanked off his leg—it was fake?—to reveal an ancient-looking peg leg. "Let's find our principal," he growled. Brady and I took a second to recover—standing in front of us was a two-hundred-year-old raging sea dog. "But first, let's get Frida and Vlad." Hey, that was our plan!

We raced to Ms. Kahlo's classroom, but all Ahab had to do was knock with a strange rhythm and she was in the hall in seconds, ready to tussle with some pirates. Brady and I must not have looked like the cleanest, most well-rested siblings of all time. She did a double take, then gave us a big, warm hug. "I'm so glad you're not hurt." Then she got that intense Ms. Kahlo look on her face. "It's time to show that pirate why you don't mess with the faculty here."

"Um, Ms. Kahlo," I said, raising my hand dumbly.

"I don't know if we're a match for fifteen pirates, but I think we know someone who is. Where can we find..." I cleared my throat. "Don Quixote?"

"Don Quixote?" she replied, like I'd said a hilarious joke. She and Ahab gave each other a look and started cracking up.

"Did somebody call Don Quixote?" a voice behind me boomed. It was a tall guy in a full suit of medieval armor, steel helmet and everything, carrying a huge lance. I jumped up and cheered. Our knight! We were going to be okay! But why did I recognize that voice, and why did it not exactly fill me with confidence? The knight opened the visor of his mask. "Hola, Javier," Señor Q said.

Señor Q? I felt all my hope and confidence deflate. "Watch out, mi amigo!" he yelled, slamming his visor back down and raising his lance. "There is a troll attacking you!" He charged at something behind me with his lance and I spun around. Blackbeard summoned a troll? With a crash Señor Loco speared some kid's art class sculpture. It shattered on the floor as Q's lance hit the lockers behind it and he went flying.

"Ay, Señor Q, not again," said Ms. Kahlo, rubbing her temples.

"There's no time for your shenanigans, Q," Ahab spat. "We must get Vlad and find Gale!"

Just then we heard some gruff voices around the corner and ducked into Ms. Kahlo's classroom, Señor Q crawling in behind us, his armor clanking way too loudly.

"Don't worry, Ed. When we find the principal, and I'm made first mate in this new world, I'll dub you my first mate. First Mate's Matey. It has a nice ring to it, no? Hey, wait a second. Swords out. Do ya hear something?"

We froze in place. I swallowed my breath as I heard them draw their swords. They were probably two feet away from us, on the other side of the stairs. I could smell them. So that's what death smelled like. Basically like sewage wrapped in steaming hot garbage. It made sense, I guess. I didn't expect death to smell like cupcakes and unicorns.

"Nothing to hear but your loud breathing, Tom. Maybe it came from over there."

They headed down the hall and turned the corner.

Then I heard my new favorite voice say, "Excuse me, are you gentlemen lost?"

"Um...um, n-n-no, ma'am! We were just heading to, er...to meet with a teacher. I think her room's right over there!" Scurrying footsteps got quieter and quieter, and then some familiar footsteps approached us. Cleopatra practically floated into the classroom. Brady hugged her and we quickly explained the situation. The teachers all bowed or got on one knee as she nodded regally. Then we all dashed down the hall to find Ms. Vlad.

Ms. V was already standing outside her classroom, with a scowl that made all of her other scowls look like smiles. "I knew this would happen. Let's go wipe the smile off that pirate's face."

We set off for the pool at full speed, Señor Q's clinking armor and Cleopatra's clanging jewelry making us sound like a really bad marching band. I did the math in my head. One ninja, one warrior queen, a sea captain, an artist, a wannabe knight, a ten-year-old piano prodigy, and three kids up against fifteen of the deadliest pirates known to man. I still didn't like those odds.

"Have any of you heard of a book called *Molly Cat*?"

I asked loudly as we ran. Everyone turned to me and shook their heads. "There's a teacher here from a book called *Molly Cat*. Ring a bell?" Nothing but blank stares.

"The title was also in another language," Brady said. "The letters didn't even make sense, they were curvy and squiggly and had dots on them."

"Probably Arabic," Ms. Kahlo said between breaths. She furrowed her brow like she was solving a crossword puzzle. "Molly Cat—the *Mu'allaqāt*! Mr. Antar!" she yelped, snapping her fingers. "Our high school poetry teacher. He would be very helpful right now. How did you know that? Forget it, there's no time. Ahab, I'll ask the office to page him and catch up with you in a minute." A famous poet? Fat lot of good that was going to do us.

We hit the high school and raced down a stone spiral staircase that got darker and darker as I got dizzier and dizzier. Finally we got to the bottom. Finistere's basement. It was time to get our butts beaten by pirates.

35

Finistere's pool is in the castle's basement.
(Do castles have basements? Well, it's underground.)
It's humongous, it's lit by torches on every side, and it's
got to be one of the raddest pools out there. It feels like
you're in a dungeon or a secret underground lake. The
walls are all rocky and cave-like and the ceiling is super
high, so the sounds echo wildly down there. When you
cannonball from the diving board it sounds like an
actual cannonball firing. And the water in the deep end
is so deep, no kid has touched the bottom.

Once we sprinted down the practically endless stairs,
there was a short hall that opened up into the pool area.
Ahab took the lead, dashing in as he yelled, "Surrender,

you cowardly pirates! From the heart of the inferno we've come to destroy you! For hate's sake I spit my last breath at you. I will sink your coffins to the bottom of the pool!" Wow, I knew Ahab was intense, but this was next level!

As we rounded the corner I expected to see one of two scenarios:

1. Hanzō laying waste to fifteen pirates as Kid Mozart and Wiki cheered him on.

2. Hanzō, Kid Mozart, and Wiki break-dancing around a bunch of tied-up pirates, with Hanzō doing a five-minute-long headspin as Blackbeard cried.

Not even close. We all skittered to a stop so quickly I almost fell into the shallow end of the pool. Right smack in front of us, so impossibly enormous that I got chills staring up at it, was a pirate ship floating in the giant pool. And not just any enormous pirate ship—the *Queen Anne's Revenge*—the most infamous pirate ship of all time. We'd read all about it in the library. One hundred feet long. Three hundred tons. Forty cannons. This was the frigate that gave sailors nightmares, that made people shudder when they heard its name, that caused terror when it was spotted at sea. And I could see why. It was gigantic, menacing, and packed to the brim with cannons. And did I mention it was MASSIVE?

Pirates lined the edge of the ship—way more than fifteen of them. There must have been fifty or sixty of every shape and size, but all terrifying. Where did they come from?

"So glad you could make it!" Blackbeard cackled. He was standing at the edge of the ship with a sword pointed at Principal Gale, who was walking the plank. Hanzō, Wiki, and Kid Mozart were tied up behind him. "You're just in time!"

"You're making a huge mistake," Gale called out to Blackbeard.

"I am? No, I'm afraid you made the mistake. You should've let me use the bell. Making that decoy wasn't easy, and for that you will pay. My crew will get some real satisfaction sabotaging this 'perfect' school you're so proud of. Isn't that right, boys? We'll burn it to the ground!"

The pirates cheered and Gale's eyes looked like they lit on fire. "Never," she said in a deadly whisper that carried across the pool. Then she locked eyes with Ms. Vlad and nodded.

Ms. Vlad took a few steps back from our group and looked over at Brady and me. "Did any of the pirates have long-range weapons? Like guns or bows and arrows?" Brady and I shook our heads. I definitely hadn't seen any. "Good," she said. Then she took a running start, jumped into the air, and transformed into a giant bat, shrieking wildly as she thrashed through the air toward the pirates. I knew she was a vampire! I knew it! I couldn't wait to rub it in Wiki's face for the rest of his life...if we lived past today.

"Okay, team," Cleopatra said, picking up a sword a pirate must have dropped. "While she's causing a distraction, let's get on that ship and vanquish those pirates." The teachers roared their approval and raced toward the ship. Ms. Kahlo looked at us and motioned firmly for us to stay. Fair enough. We watched the teachers race up the gangplank, harpoon, cutlass, and lance raised above them, yelling wildly as they joined the fray.

Suddenly it got super noisy—clangs, shrieks, screams, thuds. I was worried, because the teachers were still outnumbered ten to one. I motioned to Brady, and we raced over to the ship, heading nervously up the gangplank, afraid of the scene we'd see on board.

It only took a second to realize that the pirates were winning. The teachers were putting up a good defense, with Cleopatra playing general while Ahab kicked some serious pirate butt, but it would only be a few more minutes until Blackbeard's crew captured all of the teachers. There were just way too many pirates. How could I help? I scanned the scene desperately.

On the other side of the ship, Hanzō, Kid Mozart, and Wiki struggled with their ropes. Wiki motioned for Brady and me. The pirates were definitely way too focused on the teachers to notice us, so we snuck around the epic fight and headed toward them. When we got there, we started looking for the knots to untie them.

"What happened? The world's greatest ninja got captured by pirates?" I asked Wiki.

"No way—Hanzō practically beat their butts with one hand tied behind his back. But then Blackbeard put his blade to my neck and he had to drop his sword and surrender. The crew found Andy and dragged him over to Blackbeard, who forced me to ring the bell a million times, summoning these maniacs. And the ship. We're doomed. This is hopeless."

"Not yet," said Hanzō, who had somehow freed himself from his ropes. He pulled a dagger from his belt and then freed Wiki and Kid Mozart. "Stay here where it is safe," he said, and then did a double backflip into the middle of the brawl, immediately knocking down pirates left and right.

"Well, that almost evens the odds," Wiki said, staring at Hanzō in awe. Then he looked back at us. "But it won't be enough." He was right. Ahab and Hanzō were both taking down a lot of pirates, but more just seemed to sprout up all the time. "Also, why is Señor Q wearing armor?"

"Remember Don Quickie?" Brady sighed. "That's

him. He's apparently the worst knight of all time." Señor Q was wrestling loudly with the ship's mast, convinced it was a huge snake. He screamed at it in Spanish as three pirates surrounded him, scratching their heads. "We need one more hero. One who isn't completely out to lunch."

Then we heard the horse. It was galloping at full speed and the sound was getting closer, the hooves clanking on the stone floor and then stomping on the gangplank. We all turned our heads just in time to see a knight in glittering, flashy silver-and-gold armor raising an enormous spear above his head. "The cavalry has arrived!" he yelled, and charged his horse right into the middle of the fracas.

"Antar!" the teachers yelled, getting a second wind now that a real knight was on their team. The pirates all looked terrified, and the faculty used it to their advantage. Hanzō and Ahab were knocking out three pirates a second, and Ms. Kahlo and a now-human Ms. Vlad were tying them up at Cleopatra's command. Antar jumped off his horse and slashed through their ranks like a hurricane. Brady cheered loudly as Wiki and I just watched, jaws dropped. If you've never seen a famous ninja or knight at work, I highly recommend it.

Two minutes later the teachers were all lined up in a row with Principal Gale at the front. They were facing down Blackbeard—and behind him his pirate friends were all writhing on the floor, tied up.

"Drop. Your. Sword." Principal Gale said it firmly and fearlessly. It sent shivers down my spine. What a principal.

Blackbeard smiled. Uh-oh.

"Drop my sword? Gladly." He lifted the sword up high and made a big show of dropping it. "What's that line again? The pen is mightier than the sword?" He pulled a feather out from behind one ear. "I agree completely. You should have asked me to drop my feather."

Then he calmly walked over to his captain quarters, opened the door, and pulled out a tied-up teacher.

Jekyll.

Everyone looked confused, especially Jekyll, until Blackbeard tickled him with the feather.

"You call yourself a pirate?" Ahab asked Blackbeard. "What nonsense is this?"

Blackbeard held up one finger of his left hand as he tickled with his right. "Wait for it…"

Jekyll laughed and laughed and in between laughs gasped, "Stop! Please! Please don't!"

"Stop it!" Principal Gale yelled. She motioned to her teachers. "Get him."

All at once Jekyll's body began bulging—first his chest and his arms grew to monstrous size, then his legs, and finally his head morphed into the beast we were all hoping we'd never see again.

36

Hyde let out a monstrous howl. "**YEEHAW! WOW, IT FEELS GOOD TO BE OUT OF THAT PUNY CAGE AGAIN! NOW WHO'S IN THE MOOD TO PARTY? AND BY 'PARTY' I MEAN, GET BEAT UP?!**" he yelled, punching his fist into his other hand.

Everyone took a few steps back, not sure what to make of the raging-but-smiley monster.

"These teachers specifically requested a party, Mr. Hyde," Blackbeard said calmly, pointing at the faculty.

"**AW, SHUCKS, REALLY? YOU GUYS REQUESTED A HYDE PARTY? I'M TOUCHED. NOW LET'S PARTY!**"

Hyde lifted a cannon over his head and threw it

against the wall, shattering it. Then he did it again with another three cannons.

"WOO! DO I KNOW HOW TO PARTY OR WHAT?"

Everyone was still in shock over what was happening, and they were just standing there like idiots. Blackbeard didn't waste a second. "Get your friends involved too!" Blackbeard yelled to Hyde.

"OH RIGHT, HOW COULD I FORGET?" he yelled, leaping over to where the teachers were standing, frozen in shock.

"IF THIS IS A POOL PARTY, WHY ISN'T ANYONE IN THE POOL? I'M SURE THE WATER'S FINE!"

Before I had time to blink, Hyde started lobbing each teacher enthusiastically into the pool. It was a long way from the ship's deck to the water, and he threw them hard—it sounded like a bad belly flop each time. I was worried they might be seriously hurt. Then Ms. Vlad turned into a bat and he head-butted her and threw her in too.

"I JUST HEAD-BUTTED A GIANT BAT! HOW AWESOME IS THAT?!"

In no time all of the teachers were off the ship, flailing

in the pool below. Blackbeard pointed down at Andy. "Now destroy the table."

He looked back at his pirate friends. "Cross your fingers, boys. If this doesn't send us back, nothing will."

"CANNONBALL!" Hyde yelled as he took a running start, jumped a hundred feet into the air, and cannonballed right onto Andy, shattering him into a hundred pieces.

Blackbeard cackled loudly. "We're free!"

"PARTY'S OVER, EVERYONE," Hyde growled. "NOW YOU'RE STUCK WITH US FOREVER!"

"NOOOOOOOOO!" Brady let out an enormous scream, and I gasped loudly. Wiki just stared in shock.

Andy. Destroyed. All hope was lost.

I heard some deep rumbling below us as the floor shook. It felt like a little earthquake, but it only lasted a few seconds. How odd.

Then Blackbeard noticed us at the edge of the ship and laughed. "Perfect timing, lads. Hyde, I promised these kids a spectacular death. Could you help me keep my promise?"

"IT'S VERY IMPORTANT TO KEEP PROMISES!" Hyde

yelled as he bounded over to us, scooped the three of us up, and leapt down to the pool's edge. He shoved us all to the floor, hard. Then he grabbed Kid Mozart by his fancy shirt and lifted him up over his head. "NOW HOW SHOULD I KILL YOU? THERE ARE HONESTLY JUST TOO MANY CHOICES!"

I had to do something.

"Wiki!" I whisper-yelled. Wiki looked over at me, his eyes too terrified to process much. "You're right next to Hyde. I need you to kick him in the butt."

"What?! Are you out of your mind?" He shook his head so hard I thought it'd fall off.

"Wiki, for once in your life, you need to trust someone other than yourself. You need to trust me."

"No way. I mastermind the plans. This is life or death."

"No, this is just death unless you kick him in the butt right now. Wiki, trust me."

Wiki looked like he was fighting a battle in his brain.

"OKAY, OKAY. HOW DOES THIS SOUND? I THROW A PIANO DIRECTLY AT YOUR FACE." Hyde was looking for feedback, but Kid Mozart looked like he was about to die of fright. It was now or never.

"Wiki, now! Now, now, now!" I yelled. Wiki took a deep breath, closed his eyes as hard as they'd shut, and kicked Hyde smack on his left butt cheek. Hyde dropped Kid Mozart and flung himself around. For the first time ever, he actually looked angry. Boy, was this a dumb idea.

I waved. "I want to go first!"

Hyde pushed me to the ground and put one huge hand on my chest, holding me down. "OOH, REQUESTS! OKAY, THEN, LET'S START WITH YOU. HMMM, HOW SHOULD I KILL YOU?"

"Wait!" I said as he slobbered all over me.

"WHAT?!" he yelled, his eyes bulging from his face.

Okay, Javi, you have maybe three seconds to think of something. If you don't, you will die, and all the bad guys will go wreak havoc on the world. Three seconds to save yourself and save the world. No pressure.

I looked around. All the adults were out of commission. It was just Hyde and little old me. And I was so terrified, I was shaking.

Shaking! The entire room seemed to shake when Hyde destroyed Andy. What was that rumbling below? Maybe it wasn't an earthquake. Ooh, hold on. Remember the rumors, Javi. Remember what kids say lives under the school.

Okay, I had an idea. If I was wrong I'd be dead, and if I was right I'd probably be dead too, but I might save everyone else.

"Well, I...I thought of a more fun way for you to kill me."

"OH YEAH? HEY, THAT'S PRETTY SWEET OF YOU! WHAT IS IT?"

"There are a bunch of awesome medieval weapons in the basement, down there. D-d-do you like swords and spears and stuff?"

"DO I EVER! LEAD THE WAY!"

I ran over to the door that students were always afraid to open and swung it open. I glanced back and saw Brady's and Wiki's confused looks. Then I ran down the dark stairwell with Hyde barreling down the stairs behind me.

"DO THEY HAVE FLAILS? THAT'S THE SPIKY BALL AND CHAIN ATTACHED TO A STICK. I'M REALLY MORE OF A FLAIL GUY. THEY'RE JUST WAY MORE FUN."

We got to the bottom of the stairs, and the room ahead seemed to be lit by fire. Wow, it was really hot too. What was that dreadful heat about? My face felt like it was about to melt off. Well, nowhere to go but forward. We dashed into the room and—

"RRRRRRAAAAAAAAWWWWWWRRRRRRRR!!!!!!!!"

I'd seen a lot of crazy things since Andy came into our lives—giant bats, loco monsters, flying beasties. But nothing could prepare me for what smashed through the stone wall in a furious rage. It practically made my eyes explode.

A hideous creature reared up on its hind legs. It looked like a crazed, deformed dragon, but bigger. It had a huge head with bulging eyes that were literally on fire and giant fangs that looked razor-sharp. It had thick, trunk-like legs, and thinner, spindly arms—but at the end of each arm were little hands that had insanely long claws. It was easily the most terrifying thing I've ever seen, and it probably haunted everyone who saw it for life. It also reminded me of a drawing I'd seen somewhere.

The psycho-dragon spread his wings and threatened Hyde with a roar and a hiss. Then I remembered where

I'd seen it—in one of the Alice in Wonderland books Dad used to read to me. This was the Jabberwock, the most dangerous, murderous nightmare of all time! Oh, and—no big deal—Hyde freaked out, threw me at it, and I landed on this horrifying creature's neck, clutching on for dear life.

Then Hyde screamed, ran up the stairs, and the Jabberwock chased after him, crashing right through stone walls with me riding on its neck. "I'm dead!" I screamed as we crashed through the first wall. "I must be a ghost!" I screamed as we crashed through the second. "Being a ghost is highly overrated!" I screamed as we crashed through the third and final wall, flying into the pool area as everyone else screamed.

The Jabberwock must have wondered what a pirate ship was doing in the pool, because he flew straight to it and hovered above the deck, probably getting ready to give the *Queen Anne's Revenge* a taste of his fire breath. The pirates went pale, but Ahab, Ms. Kahlo, and Hanzō had just crawled back onto the deck and seemed less afraid. I guess the teachers knew this humongo horror hung out in the basement? Just as the Jabberwock breathed in, getting ready to let loose a fireball or two, I saw a familiar face step into the middle of the ship, make eye contact with the beast, and shake her head firmly. Aunt Nancy? The Jabberwock seemed to see her and flew back to Hyde. I glanced back and saw Ahab and Hanzō rushing toward the horde of distracted pirates. Welp, those weren't good odds.

The Jabberwock landed with a thunderous thud on the basement floor, right in front of Hyde, who screamed and fell onto his butt. "HEY, I'M SUPPOSED TO BE THE BIGGEST MONSTER!" he said, terrified and also... crying? "NO FAIR! NO FAIR! I'M THE BIG MONSTER!" He curled up into a ball, sobbing. "NO FAIR! NO FAIR!" He kept repeating it and slowly his body started shrinking until it was just Jekyll, who looked up to see a nightmare staring him down.

I got super excited that I'd defeated Hyde! And then, 0.3 seconds later, I realized that we now had a gargantuan, psychotic dragon-beast to defeat. Replace the monster with an even bigger monster. Classic Javi move.

"GRRRRRRRRRRRRR..." the Jabberwock growled as he turned his fiery eyes to look straight at me. Yikes. He wasn't super stoked to have a rider. I waved dumbly. He tilted his head, wondering what to do with me. Then he glared and started sucking in air. Oh. OH. Was this dumb dragon about to fry his own neck just to kill me?

"Somebody help!" I screamed. But no one seemed to be conscious on the ship.

"Hey! Hey you, beastie! Come pick on someone your own size, why don't you!" I looked down and couldn't believe my eyes. Jekyll was poking the Jabberwock's scales, taunting him. The beast looked down at him, and Jekyll smiled nervously. "Heh heh... Not to say that I'm your own size..." Then he cleared his throat and stood up straight. "But put the boy down at once! Or else...or else..."

The Jabberwock brought its head down until it was inches away from Jekyll. I could almost hear him saying, "Or else what?" Jekyll stepped a few paces back, trying not to get burned by the dragon's eyes. Oh man. Jekyll saved my life, awesomely and unexpectedly, but now what? Either the monster burned Jekyll to a crisp, or Hyde would come back and we'd be back to square one. Could someone else help, please?

"Hold tight, Javi!" Aunt Nancy yelled, running up to the monstrosity. She put her hand on the beast's neck and patted it. The Jabberwock calmed down instantly and brought its head in front of Nancy, who started whispering into its ear.

Then—*POOF!*—the Jabberwock disappeared, and I fell onto the cold floor.

37

"Aunt Nancy! We did it!" I said, giving her a big hug. "But...how did you do that?"

"You came up with the clever plan, Javi," she said sweetly. "And don't you forget it. I just told him to go home. Now you know what lives in the basement." She winked, and I felt like a million bucks for approximately two seconds, until I remembered.

"Wait—Blackbeard! We're doomed!" I raced to the ship imagining what must have happened while we were duking it out with a psychotic dragon. Blackbeard probably captured the teachers and was in the process of chopping off Kid Mozart's head. Oh no! Poor headless Mozart!

I was so in my own head that I didn't notice Aunt

Nancy chuckling as she jogged behind me. When we walked across the gangplank we were greeted by Frida and Ahab. Behind them were fifty-odd pirates tied up. But that didn't quite look like rope...

"What about Blackbeard? The pirates had the upper hand." Beardo was tied up extra tight in the middle of the ship, cursing quietly.

"Javi," Aunt Nancy said, putting her arm on my shoulder, "Don't you worry about it. The ninja took care of the pirates and the captain took care of Blackbeard. The dragon was the perfect distraction."

"Told you he wasn't a true captain," Ahab chuckled. "Just a stinking pirate."

The rest of the faculty were either getting out of the pool and joining us or on the ship and making sure the pirates were tied up tight. Antar was trotting his horse back and forth on the deck and pointing his sword at any scalawags that were getting too loud, while Hanzō and Wiki inspected an extra-large pirate. I walked over as Hanzō pulled a little bit of the rope off and studied it, showing it to us. It wasn't rope at all—more like silk or something even thinner and stickier. Weird.

"Where is Brocéliandus?" Ms. Vlad asked as she climbed up the gangplank, squeezing the water out of her hair.

Just as I was starting to feel good, I remembered. "Hyde. Hyde destroyed him." Jekyll looked at me sheepishly.

We walked over to the spot where Andy's remains were scattered. Gale, Brady, Wiki, and the teachers were standing over them, staring down sadly.

"I...I'm at a loss," Gale said quietly. "Brocéliandus..."

Brady started crying softly. Wiki's eyes were welling up with tears.

Aunt Nancy walked over to Andy, smiling. She patted Gale on the back and shook her head. "Why the tears, Dorothy? Do you think this is the first time someone's tried to destroy Brocéliandus?" She leaned over the remains of the table. "Hey B, stop being so dramatic and making everyone cry already!"

There was a whooshing noise, and it felt like all the air in the room was sucked into a vortex right in front of us. Then I noticed all the little fragments of wood trembling on the ground, jittering wildly. And all at once they magnetized together and WHISK!

There was Andy, good as new, purring louder than ever!

"Andy!" Brady yelled, jumping on him and giving him a huge hug.

"Oh, thank goodness!" Gale gasped.

Wiki and I just hollered and clapped awkwardly because we were excited and didn't know what else to do.

"That's more like it," Aunt Nancy said, winking at me. "Now let's send these jokers back to their homes."

Between the teachers and Brady's squad, we made short work of it. They plopped each pirate on Andy's chairs, and Brady insisted on ringing the bell every time, saying "Take that, suckers!" or "See you never, sewer stench!" as she banished them away.

The enormous pirate ship floating in the pool took a few minutes to figure out, but Brady put a chair on its deck, rang the bell, and the whole thing vanished. For a second she was suspended fifty feet in the air, and then she did the most epic cannonball of all time. Leave it to Brady to make anything into an extreme sport.

Blackbeard was the last to go. "You're going to leave

me to that grisly death, are you?" he asked quietly, but a little afraid.

Brady shook her head. "Stop being the world's deadliest pirate and I bet you can 100 percent avoid it." He gave her a small nod like he was actually considering it. Then she got really close and whispered in his ear, "Now find yourself another Pirate Queen, ya scurvy dog!" as she rang the bell in his face. POOF! The guy who almost murdered us a dozen times, gone just like that.

"Well done, everyone," Aunt Nancy said as she took a few steps away from the group. She waved at Principal Gale. "Until next time." Then her body stretched and mutated in front of us until she transformed into a giant spider and scuttled away on eight enormous legs. UM, WHAT? Half of us froze in shock, though none of the teachers seemed too surprised.

Wiki looked at the spider. Then at me. Then back at the spider. Then at me.

"Um, Javi... I don't know how to put this... Did my aunt just..."

"Turn into a spider?"

"Yeah."

"Yes. Yes she did. You know what? That actually explains a lot." I picked up some of the spiderweb that had tied up the pirates.

Principal Gale smiled and patted me on the back. "It's a long story, Javi."

"Maybe it's a story we can share over dinner?" Kid Mozart asked, walking up to us. "I see a dinner table that's itching for some company..."

"Oh, Kid Mozart," Brady said sweetly. "Do you ever have any bad ideas?"

38

It was midnight two Saturdays later, and Brady, Wiki, and I had fallen asleep watching sloth videos in our living room. That's when I heard the noises, faintly at first and then closer and louder. Someone knocked on our door. Then there were a bunch of different knocks from different people. Then one shout. Then a lot of shouting. I jumped up and raced to the door, opening it wide as a bunch of people marched inside. All at once I turned the lights on and they began shouting.

"Asalto! Surprise!"

Wiki and Brady shot up from their sleeping bags, Brady leaping into a full karate stance, Wiki screaming like he was getting murdered. In front of them was

Principal Gale, Aunt Nancy, Kid Mozart, Ahab, Ms. Kahlo, Jekyll, Hanzō, Mr. Bottom, Cleopatra, and Don Quixote.

They started playing the instruments I'd given them and tried their best to sing the Puerto Rican parranda song I'd taught them, but it was pretty much the worst rendition ever. Still, it didn't matter, the point was freaking out Wiki and Brady, and mission accomplished! But now Wiki and Brady were overjoyed. Brady was hugging Kid Mozart, and Wiki and Hanzō were bowing to each other.

Five minutes later we were all gathered around Andy and having the dinner party to end all dinner parties. I'd spent days secretly planning the menu, setting up the decor, and finding the perfect music. And I must say, everything was looking, sounding, and tasting pretty darn great.

"Pass the tostones, please. Is that how I should pronounce it? Toast-tone-nes?" Cleopatra asked, taking the basket of deliciousness and putting a few more on her plate.

"Exactly right," Brady said. "But that's just the second-best thing you can do with a plantain. Javi, bring out the mofongo!"

Brady was right. Tostones are actually the

second-best thing in the world. Mofongo is king. (Here's the one-sentence recipe: cut up a plantain, fry it, mash it, add garlic, and pork rind, and then stuff it with your favorite meat. Bliss!) I brought out a heaping plate of shrimp mofongo, and everyone's eyes went wide as they took a whiff of it.

"You're all far too focused on the food and not paying attention to the music," Ahab said, doing a little jig around the table. "This is my favorite sea chantey!"

"Ahab, if sea chanteys be the food of love...dance on!" Mr. Bottom proclaimed, raising his glass.

Yep, I was blasting sea chanteys. Good dinner parties have themes, and there was really only one option for the theme of this dinner party.

"Pirates!" Brady said to Kid Mozart, who'd leaned over to ask her about the decor. "See, this is pirate music, some of this food is seafood (which pirates eat), and Javi even dressed up Andy like a pirate ship." I'd made a mini mast out of a broom handle and some of my sheets. It wasn't quite the *Queen Anne's Revenge*, but it didn't look half-bad, really.

"You throw a superlative dinner party, Javi," Jekyll

declared. Yep, that Jekyll. He was my guest of honor. "I would like to thank you again for inviting me to your soiree, all of you. I apologize profusely for having to deal with my, ahem, other self, and am thrilled that you understand I want nothing to do with him."

"Hey, you did risk your life to save mine," I reminded him. "You're pretty rad in my book."

"Have you burned all the feathers in your house?" Ms. Kahlo asked. She wiggled her fingers at Jekyll like she was tickling the air and they had a good laugh.

"I would like to propose a toast," Principal Gale said, reaching for her glass as she stood up. "To Wiki, the brains; Brady, the brawn; and Javi, the imagination. Thank you for letting our humble Finistere continue its mission of becoming the greatest school in the world. And, hey—you just might have saved the world too." Wiki and I blushed. Brady curtsied.

"And this time," Aunt Nancy said, "You didn't have to call on your old friends to save the day." She winked at Principal Gale, who winked back.

Everyone clinked glasses, but I leaned over to Brady. "What was that about? Who are her old friends?"

Brady chuckled. "Have you not figured it out yet? Principal Gale. Who always wears emeralds. And has flying monkeys as pets. Have you never noticed the little toy scarecrow on her desk? Or the framed photos of her tiny dog? Who do you think her old friends are?"

"Oh," I said, eyes getting as wide as they could get. "Oh wow. Our principal is actually—"

Jekyll cleared his throat. "Now, I'm not sure about the rest of you, but I for one am very curious who our dear principal plans to summon as our next teacher."

Gale nodded. "Ah yes, I suppose now is as good a time as ever. There's need for an American history teacher in the high school, and I think I've found the perfect one. Now, nobody peek. I want it to be a surprise." She carefully placed a card on the table in front of her and stood up.

"Javi, if you would please do the honors." She smiled.

I rang the bell, and after the blinding flash of light someone very familiar was sitting in her chair.

"Rosa Parks!" Brady and Cleopatra exclaimed.

"Brady, Cleopatra, so happy we're dining again."

Everyone looked at Brady and the queen in shock.

"How exactly are you acquainted with Rosa Parks?" Principal Gale asked. Brady shrugged and gave her a look that said "long story." Then the principal turned to our new guest. "Ms. Parks, I wonder if you and I could take a walk. I'd like to talk to you about an educational opportunity."

"I would be delighted," she said, and the two of them walked out the door.

"I thought she'd want to summon more than one teacher," Wiki muttered.

Ms. Kahlo turned to him and nodded. "We have a second teacher who is going to come in and do guest lectures once a month. And I think you'll be pleased with who we've chosen."

Kid Mozart took a little bow in his seat. "I'm excited for my new position and even more excited that I will be able to visit you three regularly."

Brady, Wiki, and I stood up and clapped. "That's the best news ever!" I said.

"And how about hosting one of these dinners when I visit?" Kid Mozart asked. "I think we should do this regularly too."

"Eat dinner with this cast of characters? I can carve

out some time from my whale hunt for that," Ahab said, then muttering. "Though if this table can summon anything, I might be in luck..."

"Then it's settled—we'll invite you guys once a month. Javi can finally have the dinner parties of his dreams," Brady said.

"I already have the next theme figured out," I said.

"It better match up with my cooking," Aunt Nancy said, winking.

"I have one question for you," Mr. Bottom asked Brady as Mozart came back to the table.

"Shoot."

"If you could invite any three people to dinner, living or dead, who would they be?"

"DON'T START THAT AGAIN!" Wiki yelled and rang the bell.

With a *poof!* some of the guests vanished.

"Wiki!" Brady groaned. "We haven't even had dessert!"

Wiki pointed to the front door. Dad was opening it, his mouth open wide when he saw the dining room all decked out. Mom was behind him, eyes wider than his mouth. They'd just come back from the airport.

"What in blue blazes is going on here?" he asked, probably a tad confused that Wiki's aunt and our teachers were dining with us at a pirate ship table.

Brady shrugged. "School assignment. Want some mofongo?"

WIKI'S PEDIA

Extra intel on our visitors from Wiki's notebooks.

BLACKBEARD

The most notorious pirate ever, Edward Teach commanded a crew of hundreds as he wreaked havoc around the West Indies and along the coast of Britain's North American colonies. In 1717 he converted a captured French vessel into *Queen Anne's Revenge*, his legendary forty-gun warship. From there he terrorized what would later become the United States, capturing ships, stealing cargo, and blockading ports. Blackbeard rejected the use of violence but was a master at intimidation, wrapping slow-burning lighted coils in his hair and beard to make his face look like it was on fire. As epic as his reputation became, his reign as a dreadful pirate only lasted a couple of years. He was violently killed in 1718 by Robert Maynard, who mounted his head on the bowsprit of his ship to tell the world that Blackbeard had been defeated.

ANANSI (AUNT NANCY)

Anansi the spider is one of the most important characters in African, African American, and Caribbean folklore. Anansi is a trickster who uses cleverness or secret knowledge to fool people into doing what she wants. Often it's important things like creating the sun, moon, stars, and planets; gifting humans all the stories in the world; or bringing writing, agriculture, and hunting to Earth. Stories of Anansi began in western Africa, but the slave trade brought those stories to the Caribbean and the United States. In the US, Anansi's named changed to Aunt Nancy. (So she has the same name as my aunt. It's just a coincidence. Let's not be ridiculous.)

CAPTAIN AHAB

The fanatical captain of the whaling ship *Pequod*, Ahab dedicates his life to finding and destroying Moby Dick, the white whale that bit off his leg. On his final mission he hires a crew by fooling them into thinking they're going on a typical whaling expedition. Once at sea, he reveals his true purpose, forcing them to join his quest for revenge and offering a golden doubloon to whoever spots Moby Dick. When a crewmember finally sees the white whale, they go on a disastrous three-day chase that ends with a tragic battle. Ahab gets tangled up in his harpoon line, falls overboard, and gets dragged into the depths by Moby Dick, drowning. His story is told in Herman Melville's novel *Moby Dick*.

FRIDA KAHLO

Born Magdalena Carmen Frieda Kahlo y Calderón, Mexican painter Frida Kahlo became one of the most famous artists of the past century and a feminist icon whose popularity keeps growing. Kahlo got polio when she was six, which damaged her right leg and gave her a limp. When she was eighteen, Kahlo suffered a horrible bus accident that caused her chronic pain and medical problems for the rest of her life. Despite all of these setbacks, Kahlo became a beloved artist best known for her colorful, imaginative self-portraits that were inspired by her emotional and physical struggles.

DOROTHY GALE

Dorothy Gale is the main character of L. Frank Baum's *The Wonderful Wizard of Oz* and many other Oz books. She lives on a farm with her uncle and aunt when a tornado sweeps their house to the magical land of Oz. Just about everyone's read *The Wonderful Wizard of Oz* or seen the movie *The Wizard of Oz*, but L. Frank Baum wrote thirteen more Oz books, and other authors wrote dozens more, so Dorothy has far more adventures than taking on the Wicked Witch of the West. Dorothy eventually moves to Oz permanently, living in an apartment in Queen Ozma's palace.

DR. JEKYLL AND MR. HYDE

The main character of Robert Louis Stevenson's book *The Strange Case of Dr. Jekyll and Mr Hyde*, Dr. Henry Jekyll is a respected doctor in England who creates a potion to hide his bad side. Instead it turns him into Edward Hyde, a hideous, murderous monster. Jekyll tries controlling his alter ego, and for a while he has the upper hand, but eventually Hyde takes over, and it leads to their deaths.

DON QUIXOTE

Alonso Quixano was a noble living in La Mancha, Spain, who read so many books about knights that he lost his mind and decided to become Don Quixote, the greatest knight ever. He dusted off an old suit of armor, pretended his old horse was the great steed Rocinante, and convinced the peasant Sancho Panza to be his squire. The two spent their days fighting windmills they thought were giants and attacking sheep herds they thought were armies. His adventures are told in the book *Don Quixote* by Miguel de Cervantes, which is considered by many to be the greatest novel ever written.

WOLFGANG AMADEUS MOZART

A musical genius and one of the greatest composers ever, Mozart began composing music at the age of five and performing it for royalty all over Europe. Over the next thirty years he composed more than six hundred operas, symphonies, sonatas, concertos, and choral pieces, many of which are considered the best of all time. People still play his music everywhere and anywhere. He's a huge influence on the music we hear today.

ROSA PARKS

Known as the mother of the modern-day civil rights movement in America, Rosa Parks was a lifelong activist who taught the country that Black people should be treated equally and changed the course of history. In 1955, when Black people were still segregated (meaning they had to attend different schools, use different public restrooms, and eat in different restaurants), Rosa Parks got on a bus and refused to give up her seat for a white man. The driver called the police, Rosa Parks was arrested, and it sparked a huge protest that ended when the Supreme Court ended racial segregation on public transportation. It was an important win that helped end segregation altogether.

CLEOPATRA

Cleopatra ruled ancient Egypt for almost three decades and is one of the most famous women who ever lived. At eighteen she and her ten-year-old brother inherited the kingdom of Egypt, but she made enemies among the courtiers, and they ended her reign, exiling her. She crossed paths with Julius Caesar, they fell in love, and he made her queen of Egypt again. When he was assassinated in Rome a few years later, his military commander Mark Antony fell in love with Cleopatra. They married, had three children, and combined their armies to take on a Roman enemy. Cleopatra spoke three languages, was well read, was quite adept at scientific advances, and a great conversationalist to boot. She was also a brilliant politician, who brought prosperity and peace to a country that was in really bad shape when she inherited it.

HATTORI HANZŌ

Hanzō was a legendary sixteenth-century samurai, fighting in many historic battles and helping the leader of his clan become the ruler of Japan. He was known not only for his battle prowess, but also for his political and strategic brilliance. He commanded a unit of over two hundred samurai.

ANTAR

Also known as Antarah ibn Shaddad, Antar lived in ancient Arabia and was equally famous for being a mighty warrior and a brilliant poet. The Black outcast son of an Arab father and an Ethiopian enslaved mother,

Antar struggled to win over his father and his tribe, but gained great respect through his courage on the battle-field and mastery of poetry. His greatest poem forms part of the *Mu'allaqāt*, one of the most important Arabic books of all time.

ACKNOWLEDGMENTS

By this point you've likely asked yourself, "Who would I invite to dinner, if I could invite absolutely anyone?" This is my list, full of folks who I'm endlessly grateful to for making this book possible and for making my life significantly more wonderful.

Elana Roth Parker, my phenomenal agent, who gave this story wings.

Annie Berger, my astonishing editor, who made this book sing.

Juan Carlos, who found the magical forest that inspired this book, and then pushed me to write about it fifteen years later.

Jamie Antonisse, who unlocked Finistere.

Chris Baily, who painted while I wrote and made sure we did it daily.

Andy Marino and Jason Reynolds, who taught me what it takes to be a writer.

Ivan Askwith, whose advice and friendship kept me on this path.

Andrew Hume, Greg Babonis, Rachelle DiGregorio, Keren Albala, and Marlena Ryan, who read early drafts of this book and gave me such thoughtful crit.

Joe Prota, Taylor Piñeiro, Travis Nichols, Greg Berman, Brandt Hamilton, Peter Brauer, Marnie Thompson, Kacy Emmett, Austin Powe, Brittany Garrett, Courtney O'Donnell, Andrew Monkelban, Mike Delosreyes, Blaine Thurier, and Justin Juul, who helped with so many aspects of this book. (Hmm, I'm going to need a bigger table.)

Cassie Gutman, Jessica Rozler, Nicole Hower, David Miles, Michelle Mayhall, and the incredible Sourcebooks team, who were dream collaborators.

Fran and Jim, who read multiple drafts and were so incredibly supportive the whole way through.

Evelyn, who patiently read every draft, gave fantastic feedback, and believed in this from day one.

Julian, who graciously let me take breaks from playing trains to write this.

And most emphatically, Mami y Papi, who passed down their love of books and love of life, nurtured my imagination, and pulled that parranda prank on me once.

At this point you're thinking, "Victor, Victor, Victor... you could just call all of those people and invite them to dinner. This table breaks the laws of time and space to summon you literally anyone you want. Who would you *really* invite?"

Fair enough. Walt Whitman, Julia de Burgos, and Galadriel.

Now where did I put that bell?

ABOUT THE AUTHOR

Victor Piñeiro is a creative director and content strategist who's managed @YouTube and launched @Skittles, creating its award-winning zany voice. He's also designed games for Hasbro, written and produced a popular documentary on virtual worlds, and taught third graders. *Time Villains* is his first novel.